950

D0825468

ACCLAIM FOR BARRY LOPEZ'S

Light Action in the Caribbean

"Lopez displays his skill for description in writing that's precise, gorgeous [and] arresting." —*Rocky Mountain News*

"Reveals our comfort with work, our imperfections in love, our capacity for violence, and our longing for grace."
—*Austin Chronicle*

"Most of these brief fictions function as portals to another world; economical rather than slight, they call for careful reading and rereading, followed by quiet reflection." —*The Georgia Straight*

"The stories carry the reader through explorations of place, of time, of tradition, of memory and of self." —*The Plain Dealer*

"A tautly rich, rewarding read." —*The Denver Post*

"These are characters we know, or wish to have known. We dream to share their fortitude, their attempt at equilibrium, the magic launched from their each and every conundrum."
—*The Bloomsbury Review*

BARRY LOPEZ

Light Action in the Caribbean

Barry Lopez is the author of six works of nonfiction and eight works of fiction. His writing appears regularly in *Harper's*, *The Paris Review*, *Double Take*, and *The Georgia Review*. He is the recipient of a National Book Award, an Award in Literature from the American Academy of Arts and Letters, a Guggenheim Fellowship, and other honors. He lives in western Oregon.

BOOKS BY BARRY LOPEZ

NONFICTION

Arctic Dreams
Of Wolves and Men

FICTION

Light Action in the Caribbean
Lessons from the Wolverine
Field Notes
Crow and Weasel
Winter Count
River Notes
Giving Birth to Thunder
Desert Notes

ESSAYS

Apologia
About This Life
The Rediscovery of North America
Crossing Open Ground

Light Action
in the
Caribbean

Light Action
in the
Caribbean

STORIES

Barry Lopez

VINTAGE CANADA

A DIVISION OF RANDOM HOUSE OF CANADA LIMITED

VINTAGE CANADA EDITION, 2001

Copyright © 2000 by Barry Holstun Lopez

All rights reserved under International and Pan-American Copyright Conventions. Published in Canada by Vintage Canada, a division of Random House of Canada Limited, in 2001. First published in hardcover by Random House Canada, Toronto, in 2000. Distributed by Random House of Canada Limited, Toronto.

Vintage Canada and colophon are registered trademarks of Random House of Canada Limited.

The author would like to thank the editors of the following publications, in which some of these stories originally appeared: *American Short Fiction* ("Remembering Orchards" and "Thomas Lowdermilk's Generosity"); *The Georgia Review* ("The Letters of Heaven" and "The Mappist"); *The Gettysburg Review* ("Mornings in Quarain"); *Manoa* ("In the Garden of the Lords of War," "Rubén Mendoza Vega," and "In the Great Bend of the Souris River"); *San Francisco Magazine* ("Emory Bear Hands' Birds"); and *Story* ("The Deaf Girl"). "Stolen Horses" first appeared in *Writers Harvest 3*, edited by Tobias Wolff and William Spruill.

The author also would like to express his gratitude to the Lannan Foundation for a residency fellowship that allowed him to complete work on this book.

Excerpt from "Apology for Bad Dreams" from *Selected Poems* by Robinson Jeffers, copyright © 1925 and renewed 1953 by Robinson Jeffers, is reprinted by permission of Random House, Inc.

National Library of Canada Cataloguing in Publication Data

Lopez, Barry Holstun, 1945–
Light action in the Caribbean : stories
ISBN 0-679-31126-2
I. Title.
PS3562.O69L53 2001
813'.54 C2001-900858-9

Book design by Virginia Tan

www.randomhouse.ca

Printed in the United States of America
10 9 8 7 6 5 4 3 2 1

For
Debra

Contents

Light Action
in the
Caribbean

Remembering Orchards

In the years I lived with my stepfather I didn't understand his life at all. He and my mother married when I was twelve, and by the time I was seventeen I had gone away to college. I had little contact with him after that until, oddly, just before he died, when I was twenty-six. Now, years later, my heart grows silent thinking of what I gave up by maintaining my differences with him.

He was a farmer and an orchardist and in these skills a man of the first rank. By the time we met, my head was full of a desire to travel, to find work like my friends in a place far from the farming country where I was raised. My father and mother had divorced violently; this second marriage, I now realize, was not just calm but serene. Rich. Another part of my shame is that I forfeited this knowledge too. Conceivably, it was something I could have spoken to him about in my early twenties, during my first marriage.

It is filbert orchards that have brought him back to me. I am a printer. I live in a valley in western Oregon, along a river where there are filbert orchards. Just on the other side of the mountains, not so far away, are apple and pear orchards of great renown. I have taken from these trees, from their arrangement over the ground and from my curiosity about them in the different seasons, a peace I cannot readily understand. It has, I know, to do with him, with the way his hands went fearlessly to the bark of the trees as he pruned late in the fall. Even I, who held him vaguely in contempt, could not miss the kindness, the sensuousness of these gestures.

Our home was in Granada Hills in California, a little more than forty acres of trees and gardens which my stepfather tended with the help of a man from Ensenada I regarded as more sophisticated at the time. Alejandro Castillo was in his twenties, always with a new girlfriend clinging passionately to him, and able to make anything grow voluptuously in the garden, working with an aplomb that bordered on disdain.

The orchards—perhaps this is too strong an image, but it is nevertheless exactly how I felt—represented in my mind primitive creatures in servitude. The orchards were like penal colonies to me. I saw nothing but the rigid order of the plat, the harvesting, the pruning, the mechanics of it ultimately. I missed my stepfather's affection, understood it only as pride or gratification, missed entirely his humility.

Where I live now I have been observing orchards along the river, and over these months, or perhaps years, of watching, it has occurred to me that my stepfather responded most deeply not to the orchard's neat and systematic regimentation, to the tasks of maintenance associated with that, but to a chaos beneath. What I saw as productive order he saw as a vivid surface of exquisite tension. The trees were like sparrows frozen in flight, their single identities overshadowed by the insistent precision of the whole. Internal heresy—errant limbs, minor inconsistencies in spacing or height—was masked by stillness.

I have, within my boyhood memories, many images of these orchards, and of neighboring groves and orchards on other farms at the foot of the Santa Susanas. But I had a point of view that was common, uninspired. I could imagine the trees as prisoners, but I could not imagine them as transcendent, living in a time and on a plane inaccessible to me.

When I left the farm I missed the trees no more than my chores.

The insipid dimension of my thoughts became apparent years later, on two successive days after two very mundane observations. The first day, a still winter afternoon—I remember I had just finished setting type for an installment of Olson's *Maximus Poems*, an arduous task, and was driving to town— I looked beneath the hanging shower of light green catkins, just a glance under the roof-crown of a thousand filbert trees, to see one branch broken from a jet-black trunk resting on fresh snow. It was just a moment, as the road swooped away and I with it.

The second day I drove more slowly past the same spot and saw a large flock of black crows walking over the snow, all spread out, their graceless strides. I thought not of death, the usual flat images in that cold silence, but of Alejandro Castillo. One night I saw him twenty rows deep in the almond orchard, my eye drawn in by moonlight brilliant on his white shorts. He stood gazing at the stars. A woman lay on her side at his feet, turned away, perhaps asleep. The trees in that moment seemed not to exist, to be a field of indifferent posts. As the crows strode diagonally through the orchard rows I thought of the single broken branch hanging down, and of Alejandro's ineffable solitude, and I saw the trees like all life—incandescent, pervasive.

In that moment I felt like an animal suddenly given its head.

My stepfather seemed to me, when I was young, too polite a man to admire. There was nothing forceful about him at a time when I admired obsession. He was lithe, his movement very physical but gentle, distinct, and hard to forget. The Chinese say, of the contrast between such strength and fluidity, "movement like silk that hits like iron"; his was a spring-steel movement that arrived like a rose and braced like iron. He was a pilot in the Pacific in World War II. Afterward he stayed on with Claire Chennault, setting up the Flying Tigers in western China. He was inclined toward Chinese culture, respectful of it, but this did not show in our home beyond a dozen or so books, a few paintings in his office, and two guardian dogs at the entrance to the farm. In later years, when I went to China and when I began printing the work of Lao-tzu and Li Po, I began to understand in a painful way that I had never really known him.

And, of course, my sorrow was, too, that he had never insisted that I should. My brothers, who died in the same accident with him, were younger, more disposed toward his ways, not as ambitious as I. He shared with them what I had been too proud to ask for.

What drew me to reflect on the orchards where I now live was the stupendous play of light in them, which I began to notice after a while. In winter the trunks and limbs are often wet with rain, and their color blends with the dark earth; but blue or pewter skies overhead remain visible through wild, ramulose branches. Sometimes after a snow the light in the orchards at dusk is amethyst. In spring a gauze of buds and catkins, a toile of pale greens, closes off the sky. By summer the dark ground is laid with shadow, haunted by odd shafts of light. With fall an elision of browns—the branches now hobbled with nuts—gives way to yellowing leaves. And light again fills the understory.

The colors are not the colors of flowers but of stones. The filtered light underneath the limbs, spilling onto a surface of earth as immaculate as a swept floor beneath the greens, and the winter tracery of blacks, under a long expanse of gray or milk or Tyrian sky, gave me, finally, an inkling of what I had seen but never marked at home.

I do not know where this unhurried reconciliation will lead. I recognize the error I made in trying to separate myself from my stepfather, but I am not in anguish over what I did. I do not live with remorse. I feel the error only with a little tenderness now, in these months when I find myself staring at these orchards I imagine are identical to the orchards that held my stepfather—and this is the word. They held the work of his hands, his desire and aspiration, just above the surface of the earth, in the light embayed in their branches. It was an elevation of his effort, which followed on his courtesies toward them.

An image as yet unresolved for me—it uncoils slowly, as if no longer afraid—is how easily as boys we ran away from adults who chased us into orchards. They were too tall to follow us through that understory. If we stole rides bareback on a neighbor's horses and then tried to run away across plowed fields, our short legs would founder in the furrows, and we were caught.

Beneath the first branching, in that grotto of light, was our sanctuary.

When my stepfather died he had been preparing to spray the filbert orchard. He would not, I think, have treated the trees in this manner on his own; but a type of nut-boring larvae had become epidemic in southern California that year, and my brother argued convincingly for the treatment. Together they made a gross mistake in mixing the chemicals. They wore no protective masks or clothing. In a single day they poisoned themselves fatally. My younger brother and a half brother died in convulsions in the hospital. My stepfather returned home and died three days later, contorted in his bed like a root mass.

My mother sued the manufacturer of the chemical and the supplier, but legal maneuvers prolonged the case and in the end my mother settled, degraded by the legal process and unwilling to sacrifice more years of her life to it. The money she received was sufficient to support her for the remainder of her life and to keep the farm intact and working.

We buried my brothers in a cemetery alongside my mother's parents, who had come to California in 1923. My stepfather had not expressed his wishes about burial, and I left my mother to do as she wished, which was to work it through carefully in her mind until she felt she understood him in that moment. She buried him, wrapped in bright blue linen, a row into the filbert orchard, at a spot where he habitually entered the plot of trees. By his grave she put a stone upended with these lines of Jeffers:

It is not good to forget over what gulfs the spirit
Of the beauty of humanity, the petal of a lost flower
blown seaward by the night-wind, floats to its quietness.

I have asked permission of the owners of several orchards along the river to allow me to walk down the rows of these plots, which I do but rarely and harmlessly. I recall, as if recovering clothing from a backwater after a flood, how my stepfather walked in our orchards, how he pruned, raked, and mulched, how his hands ran the contours of his face as he harvested, the steadiness of his passion.

I have these memories now. I know when I set type, space line to follow line, that he sleeps in my hands.

Stolen Horses

What we did was wrong, of course, and then it got out of hand, as I suppose such things often do. I knew Ed Hemas from grade school, years ago, before all this. It was his idea. He made it work a few times, and then him and Brett Stallings and Andy Pinticton thought it would work again, and that's how I got into it.

Actually, I don't remember what I thought at the time, twelve years ago. Easy money, and I didn't have any, I guess. I was drifting between high school and whatever when Ed asked and I said, Sure, I'm in.

He and Brett and Andy had done this twice already, stealing horses and hauling them across the high desert to Burns in the middle of the night, where some guy gave Ed four hundred bucks a head and loaded them on another truck. Thirty head one time, thirty-eight another. Split three ways, cash of course. You can figure it out.

Andy brought the stock truck down from the Victor Ellen place north of Madras where he worked, tractor-trailer rig. Ed and Brett, they drove Ed's pickup with a two-horse trailer. Ed scouted places around Sisters and down toward Bend where he thought he could get the horses bunched up quiet, away from the house, and then load them in the dark, where all he needed was a little plastic fencing set up, like wings on a chute into the truck. He and Brett wrangled, Andy pushed 'em up the ramp into the trailer.

It took no more than an hour, either time. They did it under a new moon, two in the morning, no one even around maybe on these 300-acre, new-money showplaces. By sunrise, they had the truck idling in a stockyard 150 miles away in Burns, and Andy had the rig back at the ranch by noon. I don't know what he told his boss about where he'd been with the truck.

The job they asked me about was a place between Sisters and Redmond, sixty head of horses. I knew there were some registered quarters in there, I'd driven by and seen them. Andy wanted a hand with loading. Ed had gotten a deal for five hundred bucks each, so that would be $30,000 four ways. I should have said no, of course, but it looked good and I didn't care at all about the people who owned the horses.

Here's where my thoughts on this start to run deep. Ed was selling the horses to a guy who trucked them back to Michigan, back to Ohio. This guy, Ramirez or Sanchez, sold them to people who'd pay a premium for horses that came, as they say, from out west, people just getting into stock market money or lottery money, lawyering or something. Inheritances. Ed thought this Ramirez guy was getting $2,000 a head. We were stealing them from the same kind of people in Oregon, people who just got them for show. I know it's not right, but justice is a strange thing, looking at it from my end. My family ranched that central Oregon country for four generations. We took the land from the Indians to start with, but then these people, they took it from us. They came in from Seattle, California, wherever, waving big money around, desperate to get some horses in and look the part. We had to sell. None of us had ever seen money like that.

I know, there's no excuse for theft, not stealing like this, just to get a little extra money and maybe smack some of these people in the face. But anger was a strong feeling, and we all had it. We wanted to fool and rile these people. They could just buy a place they knew nothing about, none of its history or even literally which way the wind blew. And they surely didn't want to be caught around any of us, no more, I guess, than my great grandparents wanted to hang around with the Molala.

No one should have been killed—I didn't even know Ed had a gun until he shot the guy. The other guy, he had no call to run Brett down, it wasn't that sort of a deal. And Ed and Andy, they shouldn't have driven off without me, but you never see these things coming. Maybe you don't want to see it.

I had met Ed and Brett that night in a restaurant in Redmond about seven-thirty. We had a few beers and some barbecue and Ed told me about the place. North side of 126, six miles out of Sisters. The horses were in a big pasture along

the highway, but there was an access road farther north running parallel, the pasture between them. The only exposure
for us, Ed said, was rounding horses up within sight of the
highway, but at two in the morning there was no traffic and if
there was, a guy could see it a long ways off and get off his
horse so he wasn't silhouetted. Ed had drawn us a map—
where the road and fences ran, where the house was. It looked
simple.

I left my pickup at the restaurant and got into Ed's Ford
with him and Brett, their horses saddled in the trailer behind
us. Andy was driving in on his own and he was there when we
pulled in along the back fence. Ed and Brett unloaded their
horses, and after Andy and I cut through the fence wire, they
rode off into the dark. Ed thought it would take him and Brett
about thirty minutes to bring the first horses in. We set up the
ramp. Andy said we'd load 'em loose. "If they got room
enough to fall down," he said, "they got room enough to
get up."

The only part of the night I recall without anger or sadness
is loading the horses. Andy and I hardly had the fencing up
before Brett came along with the first ten or twelve. We had
no light, not even a flashlight out, so they weren't easy to see,
but I knew horses well enough to know what was there. Well-
fed, spirited animals, good conformations. A couple of roans
and an Appaloosa stood out in that first bunch in the starlight,
and a bay with a roached mane. Then Ed brought up a second
bunch, about fifteen, mostly dark but a palomino and two
paints in there, I remember. Andy and I shooed them up the
ramp, which clattered and thundered under their hooves. It
was a cool night, still. I could feel the horses on my skin, their

body heat swirling around us. I could smell their shit and hear their nostrils fluttering. I felt hard muscle ripple under my hand when I clapped a hip to steer them around. I felt their tails slap my back, and caught a glint in their bared eyes. They jerked their heads and tried to lunge past us, as if they aimed to bolt through the plastic fence. Their feet drummed steady, coming toward us on firm ground, feet shot down and pulled up so deftly I heard only the rare click of two hooves. They came up like a big wind in fall cottonwoods.

We waited a good while for the third bunch. I was peering into the night, listening to the jostle and whinny behind me when I saw the headlights of a vehicle pop up, bucking across the uneven pasture.

Andy just said, "Shit!," slammed the trailer doors shut and raised the ramp. I guess he meant to drive away, but Ed's truck was in front of him and he couldn't back that trailer through the turns behind him.

For a while I stood there not knowing what had to be done. I could see Ed and Brett, cutting wildly back and forth in front of the vehicle, then I saw the big Suburban hit Brett's horse and him go down. The guy hit his brakes and dust just swallowed everything. Right then I heard a terrific crack—high-powered rifle—and then two quick, light pops from a handgun. Then it was just dust settling in the headlight beams. And silence. The next thing I saw was Ed galloping by. He yanked the horse around in the road, loaded him in the trailer, and him and Andy roared off. It took presence of mind to load that horse. I was just standing there, and they were gone, running for the highway with the lights off.

Dammit! is all I thought. Damn! Now what? The guy in the Suburban is shot, I guess. Brett's hurt, or worse. I don't want to get caught here. All I could think to do right then was turn the horses back out. I dropped the ramp, opened the doors, and flailed my arms to spook them back to the pasture. I looped a rope, quick, in the gap where we'd cut the fence wire, and was thinking I should get to Brett when I spotted a vehicle just screaming down the highway, and I ran. I snuck along through the ponderosa and sagebrush 'til dawn, all the way back to Redmond, where I got my truck.

The police put it together in no time, what with the Ellen truck being there. Andy and Ed had gone on to Burns anyway and got arrested there that night, somebody putting a few things together quickly. Brett had a broken leg, so he went nowhere after he was run over. And Ed, he did kill the guy.

As well as I can understand what happened afterward, Andy and Brett and Ed agreed to leave me out of it. My turning the horses back into the pasture made for a lighter sentence for Brett and Andy, what with the lawyers' bargaining, and they had Ed for murder, anyway.

It never made the papers that I saw, but two years after they sent him up to Pendleton, Ed got killed. Andy and Brett did six years and have been out another six now. The murder, there's no statute of limitations on that. One of them, I suppose, could still say something and they'd come after me. But I don't expect it now.

My life got different very soon after that. I moved to Florida, got a job, one I was ashamed of, selling real estate. Got a degree in finance from the University of Miami, and now I run a small business, industrial cleaning company. I have ten employees, meet a payroll, get to a few Dolphins games and am relatively happy, with two kids and all.

I've never understood the economy. I read in the Oregon papers where the guy Ed shot had made a lot of money running a vitamin-packaging business on his ranch. My wife works with Cuban refugees teaching English, $6 an hour. My father, a few years back, took what he got for a quarter-section of our family land along the Deschutes, bought a $185,000 motor home, then lost the rest of it in Las Vegas, Reno. He lives in an apartment in Salem now, on what he got for the motor home and some Social Security.

I haven't been on a horse for twelve years, but I remember riding some fine ones. We loaded some that night, and when I see the paints and bays again in my mind I feel the pounding of their feet in my thighs, their body heat on my cheeks. I suppose they all got sold after that, then moved around again, and people made more money off them. Maybe somebody rode one of 'em once in a while. I recall those horses mostly, I believe, because they're not involved in what I'm in. For them there was no place of drifting, trying to decide what would come next. I think about the four of us, young and dumb as fence posts, thinking we'd get ahead. Ahead of what? For three of us, it got very bad very fast. Ed, he paid the price, I'd say. Andy and Brett, after something like that, you're almost always going to be behind, the rest of your life. And me, I know there's that price out for me for what I did. I don't know if I'm ahead or behind. I clean people's offices now. I'm looking for no bill.

Thomas Lowdermilk's
Generosity

Thomas Lowdermilk had long hands the shape of garden trowels, as though he had been born to his work. He grew up on the Santa Rosa Reservation and then they all had moved after World War II, his parents, his sister, and two brothers, to Escondido, north of San Diego, where he married in 1957 and with his wife raised two daughters and a son. Rosamaria passed away early, at thirty-four—cancer of the lymph system. When his daughters married, they each moved to Texas, and his son followed. He had supported them all as a gardener, and he carried on this way, working at a variety of tasks with soil and trees and plants that gave him pleasure. He was a patient man, and thorough. His services, his ministrations, were sought by many people.

He employed one man, David Cordera, and boys one after another, always bright, one or two at a time, to help with the onerous and tedious work of mowing and edging so that he might concentrate on planting and tending to flower gardens, to mulching, and pruning trees. It was rumored that he contributed financially to the college education of these young men, but he did not, beyond a bonus of $100 or so at the end of the summer if the boy was going back to school.

In 1978 Thomas Lowdermilk employed a woman for the first time, and some of the things that went wrong seemed to date from that summer. She worked for him only that one time, after she graduated from high school. Her name was Lumera Sanchez. One afternoon, when they were working together in the extensive gardens of Marian Merrick, a taciturn widow of seventy-five—these were gardens thronged with roses and irises, in which Thomas Lowdermilk had planted an acre of native California wildflowers that swirled capelike in big winds that came off the ocean in the afternoon—on that day Thomas Lowdermilk had placed his hand for a moment on the small of Lumera's back to pivot past her and avoid stepping on a pile of bulbs. Mrs. Merrick, whose constant vigilance bred suspicion, detained him in the front yard at the end of the day while the girl waited in the truck. She would hate to lose him, she began haughtily, but if ever again he touched a young woman like that in her presence she would be forced to let him go.

Thomas Lowdermilk nodded blankly. He did not mention her words to Lumera or anyone else.

The following year he again hired a young woman for the summer, Agnes Littlestorm. She and a high school boy worked with him and David Cordera in a pattern, according to what had to be done at different houses. If they split up, the girl always worked with Thomas Lowdermilk. At the end of the summer, Agnes Littlestorm left for California Polytechnic State University in San Luis Obispo with $95 in her pocket from Thomas Lowdermilk. She worked for him every summer, and when she graduated with a degree in nursing in 1984 she returned home and was hired right away at Palomar Hospital in Escondido.

Two sorts of stories circulated among the people who employed Thomas Lowdermilk. The oldest stories were about how he could make salt pan bloom, or about his genius for breeding roses, or how he had brought a diseased tree back to life. These stories were connected fittingly in people's minds with stories about his generosity toward younger people, how he had helped Agnes Littlestorm, for example, stories that led to speculation about his wealth.

The other kind of story, which started after he began hiring girls graduating from high school, alluded to flaws in Thomas Lowdermilk's ways. Mrs. Merrick was the first to urge these perceptions on her acquaintances. Indeed, she fired Thomas Lowdermilk after she saw him boost a girl onto the lower limbs of one of her walnut trees. But others began to ferret from memory unresolved incidents of petty theft or to recall times when he was late, to warn their friends that Thomas Lowdermilk had changed, that he was subtle and had appetites.

Most of his clients had employed Thomas Lowdermilk for more than twenty years. They regarded him with affection, though he returned little of this. He was more self-contained than aloof, however, concentrating more on his work than on his employers' emotions. His reluctance to speak and the patience and industry with which he applied himself led some even to think him stoic, to regard him as a kind of poetic presence. The early death of his wife, the fact that his children lived far away, and stories of his generosity all contributed to this impression; and the stories told by Mrs. Merrick and her friends did not change the image these others had of him.

He himself was aware of all these stories of wealth and talent and suspicion, often through David Cordera, but it did not occur to him to explain or clarify his life to anyone, especially a stranger.

Thomas Lowdermilk rose each morning at four-thirty, worked every day but Sunday, and spent one or two evenings a week at a bar called Los Hombres del Sur in Escondido, where he drank beer and smoked small cigars with four or five friends who, like him, were employed by many people. A kind of fantasy they all indulged in was that their services as gardeners and repairmen gave them a true and also an enviable independence. They could drop any one of their clients in a moment, for any reason they chose. No one ever compromised the others by saying what each of them knew, that only Thomas Lowdermilk had this freedom. He alone was not constrained by the impressions he made on his employers.

Thomas Lowdermilk did not say to his friends that they were not as independent as he was. The illusion shored up their dignity. And he was not certain of his own independence, of its source. He viewed the people he worked for simply as occupants of the plots he gardened; and the work fed an understanding of beauty and sustained his sense of worth. In all the years of planting and cultivating, of trimming and watering and weeding, he had lost access (as he construed it) to only a handful of plots. Someone moved and the ground around the house was subdivided. Or people lost their jobs and had to economize. A man Thomas Lowdermilk regarded as deranged accosted him one day in a supermarket parking lot, leaped from his car, leaving the door ajar and the tape deck blaring, and accused him of sowing his garden "with stupid Mexican curses and Indian crap!" *"Brujo!"* the man kept shouting at him, while Thomas Lowdermilk, who did not answer a word, put the remaining bags of groceries in his truck and drove away. Only Marian Merrick had fired him for something he knew he'd done.

He loved the field he had planted with wildflowers below Marian Merrick's house, forbs he'd spent a week on his hands and knees to plant, bulb by bulb. He was devastated when he learned that she had had the field plowed under and sodded. He went to her house before sunrise one morning, trespassing, and walked back and forth over the lawn as though searching for names in a graveyard.

In the summer of 1984 Thomas Lowdermilk hired a girl named Luisa de la Paz. In the fall she went on to Pitzer College, where she majored in art. It was course work that made her parents anxious, but Thomas Lowdermilk supported her decision. He employed her the three summers she was there and gave her $125 each September when she went back. A year after she graduated, she and Thomas Lowdermilk married. Her paintings began to appear in art shows in Escondido, then in San Diego, and finally in Los Angeles. Three years after they married, she and Thomas Lowdermilk had a child.

In the estimation of his friends at Los Hombres, the birth of his daughter, Lucinda, created a problem for Thomas Lowdermilk that he had not had before. He enjoyed the company of these men, though he did not crave it. He endured their jeers when he brought Lucinda to the bar one night. "So that Luisa can paint," he explained. "And so that I can show all of you how to change a diaper."

Ignoring his humor, they tried to reason with him. An employer, they argued, does not want to be involved in what he regards as the scandalous behavior of an employee. He looked at them blankly. The men he gardened for, they continued, thought his employing young women to help him was amusing, a kind of fun to have; their wives thought his decision was courageous and right; or, like Mrs. Merrick, they were suspicious. This break with tradition by itself made no difference. Marrying young Luisa, that was something else. Certainly he could not show very much affection for her in the presence of an employer—if he kissed her passionately, he might be fired on the spot. The fact that Luisa painted, they all agreed, worked somewhat in his favor. It added to the mystery about him that people liked to make up. But having a child with Luisa, that, they thought, was going to prove very bad. They were not sure why—his age, her age—who could say. But they believed trouble would be coming.

Thomas Lowdermilk smiled at them, these men mostly his

own age, as though he were their father. "I do what I love," he said calmly. "I grow flowers at other people's homes. I make love with my wife. I spend evenings with my friends. I have gardens to show for this, a child, your companionship. How can you discuss the danger in this? These people do not care about me. Only the occasional lunatic to deal with, the man who thought I was a sorcerer. Or Mrs. Merrick.

"No one will notice," he said. "If they do, they will be happy for me."

But people were not. A woman who had never before spoken with Thomas Lowdermilk about his private affairs inquired one day whether he had sufficient employment with his other clients to cover the baby's doctor bills. He had not told her he had had a child. She gave him baby clothes he did not need, as if he were a poor man. Another woman asked him if his kind of people had the same objection to men of fifty-four marrying women of twenty-two as hers did. A man he'd worked for only a year made a lewd gesture with his hips when Thomas Lowdermilk told him his wife's age, responding to a question he meant not to answer. Two teenage boys in another family, who gawked openly at his wife's swollen breasts when she came to pick him up, would clap him on the shoulder now and say, "Radical score, Tombo," a nickname he had never heard.

Most all of this Thomas Lowdermilk was able to ignore. He quit working for one family where a pressing interest in his private life did not let up; and he felt a subtle change in his work, for he was now on guard against any inquiry—how many students had he sent to college? Was it true that Luisa had heard from the Elaine Horwitch Gallery in Palm Springs? Had his first wife died in childbirth? Did he find he had any more energy having sex with a young woman every night?

The light and air around Thomas Lowdermilk's life became more and more disturbed. He did not mention the insults or his anger to Luisa. He did not want to upset her. He feared, too, that somehow she would be angry with him. He mentioned a few incidents to his friends at Los Hombres, but even with them he was not entirely frank. The root of his worry was that for the first time in his life—that he could remember—he doubted himself. Against his will he considered whether he had married Luisa for good reason, whether, as some said, he was too old at fifty-seven to be a good father to Lucinda. He hated the way these questions now intruded upon him. And he was angry, finally, that after all these years of ignorance, people who knew nothing of him, who had never been to his home or eaten with him, were concerned, were judging him.

An avocado rancher named Angus Clipper, who lived near Fallbrook and for whom he had worked for twelve years, was as respectful and sympathetic an ear as Thomas Lowdermilk might hope for. Once, some years before, he had returned to his truck at the end of the day to find Angus Clipper holding two hoes. He saw instantly that the edges had been evened and sharpened.

"You would have done this better," said Angus Clipper, "but perhaps I have saved you some time."

Thomas Lowdermilk nodded at him with genuine appreciation. Another time Angus Clipper put a handful of Louis L'Amour paperbacks on the front seat of his truck. "A little romantic, this guy—fantasies of the West and all," said Angus Clipper with a self-deprecating shrug. "But I like him. You might."

Against his instinct, Thomas Lowdermilk returned the gesture by giving him a copy of Juan Rulfo's *The Burning Plain*. Angus Clipper thanked him the following week as though he'd been given a saddle or some other important or practical item. Thomas Lowdermilk knew then they'd made a floor both were standing on. But he could not bring himself now to pursue any conversation with him. All he could do was accept his sympathy. He knew Angus Clipper, who'd met Luisa, had heard the rumors.

Early one morning at a huge house in Rancho Santa Fe, Thomas Lowdermilk was watering a border of marigolds, inhaling an odor he loved, when the hose went limp. He turned to see a man in a dark, pin-striped suit step carefully away from the tap and continue toward him.

"Tom," said the man as he approached with an air of distress and impatience, "Petch and I are going to have to let you go. I know this is very sudden, and I will make it up to you with some sort of severance, but the truth is we—well, mostly Petch actually, this is certainly not my idea—we just can't be a party to these rumors anymore. Our daughter is being ridiculed at school—or so says her mother. I know you would never, ever approach Jennifer with the wrong idea or actually touch her, but everyone knows what happened at Marian Merrick's place—now, really, there's a bitch for you, but that's something else. Anyway, Jennifer. Petch says it looks awful when Luisa comes and you hug her, because she's so young and it's not the way you would hug her if she were your daughter, you know? And you can't go out there and explain it to everyone, what the real situation is."

Thomas Lowdermilk made no response. He held the empty hose.

"So I'll pay you for today," said the man, taking his checkbook out and twisting the cap from a fountain pen. "And—what, a month's severance? Is that fair?"

Thomas Lowdermilk didn't move.

"Great, all right," said the man. "It'll be a bitch, I can tell you, getting someone half as good as you to look after the place," he went on, leaning over to write the check out against his thigh.

That night Thomas Lowdermilk could not fall asleep. Luisa got up in the dark to tend to the baby. "I know what's troubling you," she said when she got back in bed.

"It is my own business," he answered quietly.

"No, it is our business. Do you think none of this comes to my ears? Do you think that I do not hear the stories?"

"I would have been better off if we had met years ago."

"What about Rosamaria? She wouldn't have permitted it."

"Rosamaria was a very fine woman."

"Does Mrs. Merrick," asked Luisa, "say you were pimping, that you ran Agnes and me, all of us, while we were in school, and lived on the proceeds?"

"I have not heard that one, perhaps it's coming."

"My prayer is, not before your sense of humor comes back."

"Luisa, this is not funny. I can't sleep. These people have pulled me out of my own life, the way I pull up a weed. My work is not peaceful anymore. I am always waiting, expecting to hear something stupid or ignorant."

"Go to work for other people."

"It's no good. Everyone looks at it the same, once they find out. 'Tombo,' they say. And you, they call you—"

"*Not* in this house, not in my home!" she said fiercely, turning on him.

"I'm sorry."

"Don't let these people in, Thomas." After a moment she said, "Walk away."

He stared at the ceiling. "And where am I going to go?" he wondered. He thought of setting fire to Marian Merrick's house, and then he laughed out loud at his own foolishness. He felt his wife's back arch against him, an acknowledgment.

In his despondency, Thomas Lowdermilk decided to stop working for several people who lived a long drive from his home, Angus Clipper among them. He found other clients in Escondido, but he felt angry with himself and impoverished by what he had done. Finally he did something he had never done before—he drove out to Angus Clipper's house in Fallbrook to see if he would hire him back. He learned Angus Clipper had not hired anyone to replace him, that he was trying to do the work himself. When he asked if he could go back to work for him again, Angus Clipper said yes.

"But now I have a question for you," he followed up.

"Manny Saucedo had to stop working with me. He moved back up to Fresno to take care of his family. I need someone to take over Manny's work. Can you do that?"

Thomas Lowdermilk was stunned, but he answered in an even voice. "Yes, I can do that."

"It's not full-time, Thomas. And it's a different kind of work, looking after these avocado trees. You don't have to answer now. I'd need you two or three days a week. Just tell me what you think, when you can."

"This is something of a surprise," said Thomas Lowdermilk.

"Yes, me too, actually. I didn't think of it until you drove up." He waited for Thomas Lowdermilk to say something. "Do you have my private phone number?" asked Angus Clipper.

Thomas Lowdermilk almost answered with an invitation to discuss it at Los Hombres but caught himself.

"I'll talk it over with Luisa," he answered.

"I thought you might," said Angus Clipper.

When Thomas Lowdermilk walked into Los Hombres that night, he ordered beers around for his friends. "The second round, that also is on me," he said. His friends fingered their chilled bottles in expectation, for this was a sign something had happened. Thomas Lowdermilk said, "Do you know what they say, my friends, about the energy that comes to an older man who sleeps with a younger woman?" He sipped his bottle and carefully wiped the moisture from the table in front of him. "It's not true in the way you imagine." He tried to pick up each pair of eyes. "I thought it was I who made myself an independent man. But I've seen this is not the truth. The seed was watered by Rosamaria. She was the gardener." He palmed the sweat from his beer bottle. He saw a pattern in his feelings, a rising hope. Around this he gently cupped his long-fingered hands, as if it were a moth he was lifting from a flower. "Now it has been watered again."

The men looked thoughtful, David Cordera, his brother-in-law Miguel Escalante, and the others; and they were silent. Thomas Lowdermilk's urge at that moment was to speak of his wife's paintings, but he let it pass. "Felipe," he said instead, "your loan from Bank of America. Where does it stand now? Tell us the story."

Felipe looked around the table, and then with a philosophical shrug began to tell them the most recent news.

In the Garden of
the Lords of War

One hundred and twelve years after the Universal Holocaust, in the natural deserts of what was once western China, the Dobrit practice of staying War had reached a plateau of refinement. The Four Lords, nameless men chosen by a council of women, moved from season to season in cycles regular as the Once migration of birds, and there attained a Lyric Passage, the harmonics of stability.

In countries I had walked through in the preceding six years—Beywan, Cruel, Muntouf, and tiny Begh on the Yellow Sea in old Manchuria—I found consistent agreement at all levels of society on the worth of the Four Lords and their Rule. It was my privilege as a Wenrit scribe and a Deformed to visit the Garden of the Lords of War. Now, I convey that story, another given me on a Witness Path to the

Black Sea, along which, by every country, I have been given Safe Passage.

The Circle of Women for the Study, with whom I apprenticed for five months, numbered thirteen. The youngest was maturely fifteen, the eldest eighty-one. My apprenticeship occurred at irregular hours during the winter and spring moons. I occupied one chamber, alone, adjacent to a central meetinghouse. It was made clear that I should always be available to listen when the women told stories or during the preparation of food. When the women convened to discuss the Cultures and Texts to be presented the Lords, I was sent out into the city. I memorized thirty-four of my tutors' stories in this apprentice time, good by their account. The women were always gentle in instructing, but strict that my accent and inflections should not interfere in the Music.

I will transcribe these stories into my Given Pattern when I one day arrive at the Black Sea, the fourth, now, of the books of my Sent Journey.

The Garden of the Lords of War is surrounded by a wall three times my height. It is woven of peacock feathers in such a way as not to impede the movement of air but to be opaque to passersby. The four walls do not meet squarely at corners but in round, enclosed spaces, roofless, inside each of which stands an attendant's small house. In the outer wall at each corner is a Gate of Admission. Within, a Gate of Entry opens to stretches of wild grass, gardens of flowers and vegetables, the separate houses of the Four Lords, large pine and laurel trees, and small plots of maize, beans, and wheat. Of course, it is not permitted either to view or to speak with the Lords, so

I can only offer an impression, based on the testimony of the Circle of Women for the Study.

Most often, men in their late twenties are chosen as Lords, and it is rare for one to serve past his middle forties. The unvarying criteria for selection are as follows: (1) a man must never have taken a human life, for any reason; (2) he must never have struck or in any way harmed a woman; (3) he must be Dobrit, though I was told this designation refers to spiritual and philosophic temperament, not ethnic origin; (4) he must have raised children not his own. Finally, he must read with perfect fluency in at least three languages. Added to these criteria are some requirements of a more general nature. To be considered at all, a man must be formally recommended by an aunt, and then an uncle must compose the Story of his life and recite it before the council of women and all the Dobrit. At this presentation, any person may object to his appointment. With cause, following deliberation, the candidate might no longer be considered.

After his selection, a man begins his time of service by becoming an attendant. It is his responsibility to prepare meals for the Lords, to see to the plots, orchards, and gardens in the interior, to the pathways and a wood lot, and to assist those people chosen to change the Texts. (These are always young women and men from among the Dobrit, chosen Word of Mouth, who study under the Circle of Women before performing their duties four times a year, at Change of Season.)

From the outside, the houses of the Lords resemble one another closely, though slight differences in construction, for instance in the mortise and tenon of framing, were apparent to me. Each house sits just off the ground on chestnut posts and is girt by a veranda. Sliding walls, inset with carved cypress panels, open all around onto the porch. The low-pitched shed roofs, composed of long, half-round tiles, slope outward. Inside, the four trapezoidal rooms converge on an open courtyard. These rooms are identical, each spacious enough to contain two or three large tables (upon which rest the Texts), a sleeping mat, or futon, and a small serving table. A flat chest for clothing, several wood chairs, and a washstand complete the furniture. A slate apron in the center of each floor surrounds a small firepit. Firewood is ricked on the porch outside, an ash bucket sits opposite on a tile. From two corners of the roof, chains lead to rain barrels.

The day I was admitted to the Garden of the Lords of War was in the fourth week of spring. Many of the trees were in blossom, vegetable gardens were budding with early onions and two types of lettuce, and the flower plots were effulgent with carmine, lavender, and sulfurous blooms. I walked with two of my hosts, an older woman named Kortathena and a girl about eighteen called Marika, and with the attendant at whose gate we had entered. It was a visit of only three hours but we walked leisurely through the grounds—time enough for me to see well how closely tended they were, and to observe that though the design of the pathways and the placement of the gardens suggested symmetry, they were not so laid out. Some of the pines were of such great size I felt the area must have been sacred to others before the Dobrit arrived. Certainly nowhere have I ever seen so many spiders or butterflies, or heard so many sorts of birdsong—five altogether.

The arrangement of the Prayer among the Lords of War is

as follows: each Lord lives the whole of a season in a single room of the house he occupies. At Change of Season he moves across the courtyard to another room, which has been prepared with a fresh set of Texts and drawings, and enhanced with artwork—textiles, sculpture, and paintings. He remains there until the following seasonal change, reading and studying. This practice and sequence permitted me to view each type of room empty, though I was able to step into only two houses. (The design of these rooms is similar from house to house, though I was told the four styles of design found in each house are not meant to correspond to the seasons. The rooms are commonly called by the color of the glazed pottery on which meals in that room are served: ocean green, lantern red, Persian blue, poppy yellow.)

When a room is occupied by a Lord, it is also vased with flowers and contains a pair of birds, doves usually, though sometimes crows. A lute, *shamisen,* or other stringed instrument is present, and small bowls of spice—ginger, cinnamon, sage, vanilla bean, clove—are set about. When a room is not occupied, it appears hollow and spare. The one bright spot of color is the stack of glazed dishes on the meal table.

In the Ocean Green room I was shown, the floor was of quartersawn tulipwood, light-colored, straight-grained, with a matte sheen, as if holystoned. The long outer wall of sliding cypress panels was complemented by a taller cypress wall facing the courtyard, constructed to admit light and air in the same way. The interior walls were of unfaced stone. In the Ocean Green room, each was a single piece of micaceous granite. As well as I could guess, these massive but consoling walls were founded first and the rest of the house then built around them. How they were erected or squared I could not imagine. As was true elsewhere in this prefecture, a question was received as an impolite gesture, a condition under which I chafed, but only slightly. I was content to see and listen.

I was informed that in the Ocean Green room the evening meal was always the flesh of a winged animal.

From the Ocean Green room I was walked through a round orchard of loquat trees to see a Lantern Red room. The floor here was of clear larch, the walls of charcoal-gray basalt. The evening meal was the meat of a grazing animal. The empty basin of the hearth, the absence of candle stands, contributed to a feeling of repose or suspension in these rooms. On our way from there, in a southern portion of the grounds, we passed the entrance to a Poppy Yellow room, pointed out through a single lattice row of kumquat. Its dark floor was of mahogany and the pale walls were of a fossiliferous sandstone. The evening meal there, it was explained, was of vegetables, intentionally bland. The final rooms, the Persian Blue rooms, had floors of *li* oak. The outer wall of the one we walked up to was standing open and I saw within walls of brindled marble, the color of a flock of pigeons. The evening meal here was of carp or other freshwater fish.

In the courtyard of each house the Lords grow some flowers and vegetables, as they are inclined.

I was not permitted to look into any room that was in use— a Lantern Red room in one house, two Poppy Yellow rooms in other houses—so again must rely for these descriptions upon my companions. When a Lord steps into a new room at Change of Season, he finds lying neatly upon the tables several dozen bound and unbound Texts (in the Dobrit and other languages), along with dictionaries, paper, and pencils. The books, manuscripts, and folios of drawings all bear on a single culture—here my younger host volunteered that the Lords were then reading, respectively, of Quechua, Tomachan, French, and Xosha peoples. It is the determination and desire of each Lord to have at the end of three months enough of an understanding of the culture in which he is reading to be able to make up a single story, one that gives evidence of his study and reflects his respect, but demonstrates no enthrallment. On each of the four evenings before Change of Season, the Lords gather at the center of the gardens to listen to one story each night, recited before a fire kept by two of the attendants. When the Circle of Women speaks of the Prayer, it is to these stories told at the end of each season that they are referring.

My hosts pointed out that the Texts are not chosen solely on the basis of impeccable scholarship but consist, instead, of a variety of printed materials—novels, treatises on natural history, biographies of politicians, works of reference, ethnographic documents, hydrographic records, works of architectural theory. It is, too, a collection chosen to match the strengths in language and metaphor of an individual Lord.

I chanced here one question: Were the stories the Lords told ever written down? No, the stories were only spoken once, said my elder host. She said, further, that in their reactions to the stories, the Lords tried to reinforce in one another a desire to do well. And it was this desire—to perform their tasks well, to read carefully, to give in to the manuscripts, to think deeply—as much as the Litany of Respect that the Lords produced, she believed, that kept War at bay.

As we walked toward the Gate of Entry, my younger host

suggested I might wish to be alone for a few moments. I was grateful for her kindness, and walked some steps back along our gravel path to sit on a ginkgo-wood bench. In my six years of travel, I knew I had never before been in a place so peaceful, so eloquent. The evidence of turmoil to be found in each country, including the one I was then traveling in, was here absent. By virtue of their ferocious concentration and expertise, the architects and builders of this garden had made all that line, shade, and color might do to compose the soul work, as if a terrified animal could be calmed completely and solely by what the eye beheld.

I ran my fingers along the precise joinery of the ginkgo-wood bench, a plan of assembly that let the various pieces of wood expand and contract in the rain and sun but that did not compromise the bench's strength, its sturdiness. The alignment, the proportions, and the forgiveness of the joinery were exquisite.

I caught up to my companions at the attendant's house. As we turned together for the outer gate I said—if it would be permitted—I had one other question. How was it determined when a man was no longer fit to be a Lord of War? My elder host said that from time to time a woman in the Circle would visit a Lord and they would make love. The woman would sense a man's interior land in this way. She would discern in the act of love whether the man was gentle or not, if he was passionate and curious, whether he was generous. These men, said my host, longed sometimes, like everyone, to be with children, to occupy a less strenuous station. When a woman detected a shudder of hesitation in the emotions of love, she knew it was time to open a path for a Lord to return. The choice was the man's to make, but out of gratitude and simple respect the women did all they could to make this possible.

When a Lord is ready to return to the city, I learned, the four attendants secure the grounds and depart. The other Lords prepare a meal they all then share, using vegetables and edible flowers from their personal gardens. Afterward the three Lords begin walking their longtime companion through the grounds, playing their stringed instruments and each singing the phrases he recalls from all the stories the man has told in his years there. They walk and sing through the night. Just at dawn, before the city is astir, the Lord sets forth, passing through the outer gate and returning to the house that once was his only home. It has been kept undisturbed and now has been readied for him. After this, no one may inquire of him what he has done or what he thinks or feels. He plays a lesser or greater role in the affairs of the city, as he sees fit.

Some men, said my elder host, became again merely threads in the fabric of the community, and this, too, she thought, starved, angered, and humiliated the dogs of war.

Emory Bear Hands' Birds

My name is Julio Sangremano. I was at the federal prison at Estamos, California, when the incident of the birds occurred, serving three to five for computer service theft, first offense. This story has been told many times, mostly by people who were not there that day, or by people who have issues about corruption in the prison system or class politics being behind the war on drugs, and so on. The well-known Mr. William Hanover of the Aryan Brotherhood, he was there, and also the person we called Judy Hendrix; but they sold their stories, so there you're talking about what people want to buy.

I didn't leave that day, though I was one of Emory's men. Why I stayed behind is another story, but partly it is because I could not leave the refuge of my hatred, the anger I feel toward people who flick men like me away, a crumb off the table. Sometimes I am angry at people everywhere for their stupidity, for their buying into the American way, going after so many products, selfish goals, and made-up desires. Whatever it was, I stayed behind in my cell and watched the others go. The only obligation I really felt was to the Indian, Emory Bear Hands. Wishako Taahne Tliskocho, that was his name, but everyone called him Emory and he didn't mind. When I asked him once, he said that when he was born, his fists came out looking like bears. He was in for theft, stealing salmon. Guys who knew the history of what had happened to the Indians thought that was good; they said it with a knowing touch of irony. Emory, he didn't see himself that way.

I was put in his cell block in 1997 when I went in, a bit of luck, but I want to say I was one of the ones who convinced him to hold the classes, to begin teaching about the animals. Emory told us people running the country didn't like wild animals. They believed they were always in the way and wanted them killed or put away in zoos, like they put the Indians away on reservations. If animals went on living in the countryside, Emory said, and had a right not to be disturbed, then that meant the land wouldn't be available to the mining companies and the timber companies. What they wanted, he said, was to get the logs and the ore out and then get the land going again as different kinds of parks, with lots of deer and Canada geese, and lots of recreation, sport hunting and boating.

I'd never heard anything like this, and in the beginning I didn't listen. Wild animals had nothing to do with my life. Animals were dying all over the place, sure, and for no good reason, but people were also dying the same. I was going with the people. Two things, though, started working on my mind.

One time, Emory was speaking to a little group of five or six of us, explaining how animals forgive people. He said this was an amazing thing to him, that no matter how much killing and cruelty animals endured—all the songbirds kids shot, all their homes plowed up for spring planting, being run over by cars—they forgave us. In the early history of people, he said, everyone made mistakes with the animals. They took their fur for clothing, ate their flesh, used their skins to make shelters, used their bones for tools, but back then they didn't know to say any prayers of gratitude. Now people do—some of them. He said the animals even taught people how to talk, that they gave people language. I didn't follow that part of the story, but I was familiar with people making mistakes—animals getting killed in oil spills, say. And if you looked at it the way Emory did, also their land being taken away by development companies. It caught my interest that Emory believed animals still forgave people. That takes some kind of generosity. I'd wonder, when would such a thing ever end? Would the last animal, eating garbage and living on the last scrap of land, his mate dead, would he still forgive you?

The other thing that drew me in to Emory was what he said about totem animals. Every person, he told us, had an animal companion, a sort of guardian. Even if you never noticed it, the animal knew. Even when you're in prison, he said, there's an animal on the outside, living in the woods somewhere, who knows about you, and who will answer your prayers and come to you in a dream. But you have to make yourself worthy, he said. You have to make a door in yourself where the animal can get through, and you have to make sure that when the animal comes inside that way, in a dream, he sees something that will make him want to come back. "He has to feel comfortable in there," Emory said.

Emory didn't say all this at once, like you'd read in a book, everything there on the page. If someone asked him a question, he'd try to answer. That's how it began, I think, before I got there, a few respectful questions. Emory conducted himself in such a way, even the guards showed him some respect. He wouldn't visit with the same people every day; and when guys tried to hang with him all the time, he discouraged it. Instead, he'd tell people to pass on to others some of the animal stories he was telling. When someone was getting out, he'd remind them to be sure to take the stories along.

The population at Estamos was changing in those days. It wasn't quite like the mix you see on the cop shows. Most everybody, of course, was from the street—L.A., Fresno, Oakland—and, yeah, lot of Chicanos, blacks, and Asians in for the first time on drug charges. And we had hard-core, violent people who were never going to change, some difficult to deal with, some of them insane, people who should have been in a hospital. The new element was people in for different kinds of electronic fraud, stock manipulations, hacking. Paper crime. I divide this group into two types. One was people like me who believed the system was so corrupt they just wanted to jam it up, make it tear itself apart. I didn't care, for example, about selling what I got once I broke into Northrup's files. I just wanted to scare them. I wanted to hit them right in the face. The second group, I put them right in there with the child molesters, the Jeffrey Dahmers. Inside traders, savings and loan thieves who took money from people who had nothing, people who got together these dime-a-dozen dreams—Chivas Regal for lunch, you know, five cars, a condo in Florida. Every one of them I met was a coward, and the cons made their lives miserable. Of course, we didn't see many of these real money guys at Estamos.

We had the gangs there, the Aryan Brotherhood, Crips, Dragons, Bloods, all the rest. These could be very influential people, but the paper and electronic criminals, the educated guys, almost all white, they passed on it. If one of these guys, though, was a certain type of individual to start with, he might help a gang member out. Even mean people. Even not your own race. Prepare their appeals, lead them through the different kinds of hell the legal system deals you.

Emory, who was about fifty, was a little bit like those guys. He spoke the same way to everyone, stayed to himself. Even some of the Aryan brothers would come around when he talked. The only unusual thing I noticed was a few of the more educated whites made a point of ignoring Emory. They'd deliberately not connect with him. But there were very few jokes. Emory was the closest thing to a real spiritual person most of us had ever seen, and everybody knew, deep down, this was what was wrong with the whole country. Its spiritual life was gone.

When I first asked Emory about teaching, he acted surprised, as though he thought the idea was strange, but he was just trying to be polite. My feeling was that by telling stories the way he could, he was giving people a way to deal with the numbness. And by identifying with these animal totems, people could imagine a way over the wall, a healing, a solid connection on the outside.

Emory declined. He said people had been telling these stories for thousands of years, and he was just passing them on, keeping them going. Some of the others, though, talked to him about it, kept bringing it up, and we got him to start telling us, one animal at a time, everything he had heard about that animal, say grizzly bears or moose or even yellow jackets. Some guys wanted to learn about animals Emory didn't know about, like hyenas or kangaroos. He said he could only talk about the ones he knew, so we learned about animals in northern Montana where he grew up.

Emory spoke for about an hour every day. The guards weren't supposed to let this go on, an organized event like this, but they did. Emory would talk about different kinds of animals and how they were all related and what they did and where they came from—as Emory understood it. Emory got pretty sophisticated about this, and we had some laughs too, even the guards. Sometimes Emory would imitate the way an animal behaved, and he'd have us pounding on the tables and crying with laughter, watching while he waddled along like a porcupine or pounced on a mouse like a coyote. One time he told us there was so much he didn't know, but that he knew many of these things had been written down in books by white people, by people who had spoken to his ancestors or by people who had studied those animals. None of those books were in the prison library, but one of the guards had an outside library card, and he started bringing the books in so Emory could study them.

For a couple of months, a long time, really, it went along like this. People wanted to tell their own stories in the beginning, about hunting deer or seeing a mountain lion once when they were camping. Emory would let them talk, but no one had the kind of knowledge he had, and that kind of story faded away. The warden knew what Emory was doing and he could have shut it right down, but sometimes they don't go by the book in prison because nobody knows what reforms people. Sometimes an experiment like this works out, and the warden may get credit. So he left us alone, and once we knew he was going to leave Emory alone our wariness disappeared. We could pay attention without being afraid.

That tension came back only once, when Emory asked if he could have a medicine pipe sent in, if he could share the pipe around and make that part of the ceremony. No way, they said.

So Emory just talked.

Two interesting things were going on now. First, Emory had drawn our attention to animals most of us felt were not very important. He talked about salamanders and prairie dogs the same way he talked about wolverine and buffalo. So some guys started to identify with these animals, like garter snakes or wood rats, and not with wolves. That didn't make any difference to us now.

The second thing was that another layer of personality began to take hold on the cell block. Of the one hundred and twenty of us, about sixty or sixty-five listened to Emory every day. We each had started to gravitate toward a different animal, all of them living in this place where Emory grew up in Montana. Even when we were locked up we had this sense of being a community, dependent on each other. Sometimes in our cells at night we would cry out in our dreams in those animal voices.

I identified with the striped skunk, an animal Emory said

was slow to learn and given to fits of anger and very independent in its ways. It is a nocturnal creature, like me. When I began dreaming about the striped skunk, these dreams were unlike any I had had before. They were long and vivid. The voices were sometimes very clear. In most of these dreams, I would just follow the skunk, watching him do things. I'd always thought animals like this were all the time looking for food, but that's not what the skunk did. I remember one winter night (in the dream) I followed the skunk across hard crusted snow and along a frozen creek to a place near a small treeless hill where he just sat and watched the stars for a long time. In another dream, I followed the skunk into a burrow where a female had a den with two other females. It was spring, and there were more than a dozen small skunks there in the burrow. The male skunk had brought two mice with him. I asked Emory about this, describing the traveling and everything. Yes, he said, that's what they did, and that's what the country he grew up in looked like.

After people started dreaming like this, about the animals that had chosen each of us (as we understood it now), our routine changed. All the maneuvering to hold positions of authority or safety on the cell block, the constant testing to see who was in control, who was the most dangerous, who had done the worst things, for many of us this was no longer important. We'd moved into another place.

Emory himself didn't make people nervous, but what was happening to the rest of us now did. The guards, just a little confused, tried to look tougher, figure it out. Any time you break down the tension in prison, people can find themselves. The gangs on our block, except for the Aryan Brotherhood, had unraveled a little by this time. People were getting together in these other groups called "Horned Lark" and "Fox" and "Jackrabbit." Our daily schedule, of course, never changed—meals, lights out, showers—but all through it now was this thing that had gotten into us.

What was happening was, people weren't focused on the prison routine anymore, like the guards playing us off against one another, or driving each other's hatred up every day with stories about how we'd been set up, who was really to blame, how hard we were going to hit back one day. We had taken on other identities, and the guards couldn't get inside there. They began smacking people around for little things, stupid things. People like Judy Hendrix, who thrived on the sexual undercurrents and the brutality on our cell block, started getting violent with some of their clients. The Aryan brothers complained Emory had stirred up primitive feelings, "African feelings," they called them. Their righteousness and the frustration of the guards and the threat of serious disruption from people like Judy Hendrix all made Emory's situation precarious.

One day the story sessions just ended. They moved Emory to another cell block and then, we heard, to Marion in Illinois. With him gone, most of us fell back into the daily routine again, drifting through, trying to keep the boredom at bay. But you could hear those dream calls in the night still, and people told stories, and about a month after Emory left one of the guards smuggled the letter in from him that everybody has heard about, but which only Emory's people actually read. And then we destroyed it. He told us to hold on to our identities, to seek the counsel of our totem animals, to keep

the stories going. We had started something and we had to finish it, he said. By the night of the full moon, June 20th, he
wrote, each one of us had to choose some kind of bird—a
sparrow, a thrush, a crow, a warbler—and on that night,
wherever he was, Emory was going to pray each of us into
those birds. We were going to become those birds. And they
were going to fly away.

There were some who accepted right away that this was
going to happen and others who were afraid. I would like to
say that I was skeptical, but I was one of those who was afraid,
a person for whom fear was the emotion on which everything
else turned. I could not believe.

We got the letter on the fourteenth of June. The beatings
from the guards, with people like Hanover and Judy Hendrix having a hand in it, none of that affected the hard-core
believers, the guys they put in solitary. Especially not them.
In solitary they'd turn themselves into the smallest birds, they
said, and walk under the doors.

In that week after the letter came, a clear line began to
divide us, the ones who were leaving, the ones who were
going to stay.

The night of the twentieth, about eight o'clock, sitting
around in the TV room, I was trying to stay with a game show
when a blackbird landed on the table. It cocked its head and
looked around the way they do. Then I saw a small flock of
birds like finches out in the corridor, swooping up and landing
on the hand railings on the second tier. A few seconds later
the whole cell block was full of shouting and birdsong. The
alarms started screaming and the guards stormed in. They
beat us back into our cells, but by then birds were all over the

place, flying up and down, calling out to the rest of us. My cellmate, Eddie Reethers, told me he was going to be a wild pigeon, a rock dove, and it was a pigeon that hopped through the bars and flew past me to the window of the cell. He kept shifting on his feet and gazing down at me, and then he stepped through the bars out onto the ledge and flew away. I ran to see. In the clear air, with all that moonlight, I could see twenty or so birds flying around. I jumped back to the cell door. As many were flying through the corridor, in and out of the cells. The guards were swinging away at them, missing every time.

Five minutes and it was all over. They shut the alarms off. The guards stood around looking stupid. Seventy-eight of us were at the doors of our cells or squeezed up against the bars of the windows, watching the last few birds flying off in the moonlight, into the darkness.

In the letter, Emory told us the birds would fly to Montana, to the part of northern Montana along the Marias River where he grew up, and that each person would then become the animal that he had dreamed about. They would live there.

In the Great Bend
of the Souris River

My father, David Whippet, moved a family of eight from Lancaster, in the western Mojave, up onto the high plains of central North Dakota in the summer of 1952. He rented a two-story, six-bedroom house near Westhope. It was shaded by cottonwoods and weeping willows and I lived in it for eleven years before he moved us again, to Sedalia in central Missouri, where he retired in 1975. I never felt the country around Sedalia. I carried the treeless northern prairie close in my mind, the spine-shattering crack of June thunder—tin drums falling from heaven, Mother called it—an image of coyotes evaporating in a draw.

I went east to North Carolina to college the year Father moved us to Missouri. When my parents died, within a year of each other, my brothers and sisters sold the Sedalia house. I took no part of the proceeds. I looked back always to the broad crown of land in Bottineau County that drained away into the Mouse River, a short-grass plain of wheat, oats, and barley, where pasqueflower and blazing star and long-headed coneflower quivered in the summer wind. I came to see it in later years as the impetus behind a life I hadn't managed well.

That first summer in North Dakota, 1952, the air heated up like it did in the desert around Lancaster, but the California heat was dry. This humid Dakota weather staggered us all. I got used to the heat, though the hardest work I ever did was summer haying on those plains. I'd fall asleep at the supper table still itching with chaff. I grew to crave the dark cold of winter, the January weeks at thirty below, the table of bare land still as a sheet of iron. Against that soaking heat and bone-deep cold the other two seasons were slim, as subtle and erotic as sex.

Considering my aspirations at the university in Chapel Hill—I majored in history, then did graduate work in physics—the way my life took shape seemed not to follow. The summary way to state it is that I became an itinerant, a wanderer with an affinity for any kind of work to be done with wood. I moved a lot—back to California from North Carolina, then to Tucson for a while before going to the Gulf Coast, Louisiana—always renting. After that, I worked in Utah for six years, then moved to eastern Nebraska. I considered moving to North Dakota, but that country seemed better as a distant memory. I felt estranged from it.

Over those twenty years of moving around I installed cabinets and counters in people's homes, made fine furniture, and built a few houses. In my notebooks, dozens of them, I wrote meticulous descriptions of more than a hundred kinds of wood, detailing the range of expression of each as I came to know it. I wrote out how these woods responded to various hand tools. In line after neat line I explained the combinations of human desire, material resistance, and mechanical fit that made a built object memorable. I was in my thirties before I saw what I'd been straining after in North Carolina, obscured until then by academic partitioning: the intense microcosm of history that making a house from a set of blueprints becomes; and the restive forces involved in physical labor. It becomes apparent in wiring a house or in routing water through it that more than gravity and the elementary flow of electrons must be taken into account. The house is alive with detour and change. Similarly with squaring its frame. The complex tensions that accumulate in wood grain affect the construction of each house. Nothing solid, I learned, can ever be built without shims.

Aging got me down off roofs by the time I was forty. Pride, I have to think, a desire to publicly acquit myself by choosing a settled and respectable calling, precipitated my first purchase of a house, in Ashland, Nebraska, in 1986. Attached to it was a spacious workshop in which I intended to build cabinets and hardwood tables and chairs for the well-to-do in Omaha and Lincoln. I also found for the first time since a divorce ten years before—and not incidentally, I think—an opportunity for long-term companionship. The money was good. A year into it I felt steady and clear.

It was faith and not nostalgia that eventually sent me up to Bottineau County. The harmonious life I'd found with Doreen, a tall, graceful woman with a gift for design and for the arrangement of things, was disturbed by a single, insistent disaffection. Neither human love nor her praise for what I did could cure it. I had not, since I'd left North Dakota, felt I belonged in any particular place. During the first years in Nebraska I'd reasoned I could settle there permanently if it hadn't been for an entity still missing, like a moon that failed to rise. If I found a place to attach myself in North Dakota, I would muse, I'd stand a chance of bringing all the pieces of myself together in a fit that would last. It did not have to be a life lived in North Dakota, but if I didn't go back and see, I'd forever have that emptiness, the phantom room in a house.

The drive up to Bottineau County from Ashland takes two days. In the fall of 1991 I spent a week crisscrossing farmland there in the hold of the Mouse River, trailing like a lost dog in the big bend the river makes north and east of Minot. Not finding, or knowing, what I wanted, I finally drove up to Cedoux in Saskatchewan, where the river heads in no particular place and where it is known by its French name, the Souris. The river bears east from there, passing near small towns like Yellow Grass and Openshaw before turning south for North Dakota.

That's all the distance I went that first year.

I went back the next spring to the same spot and followed the river southeast to Velva, North Dakota, traveling slowly, like a drift of horses. The river swings back sharply to the northeast there, the bottom of its curve, and picks up the Deep River west of Kramer. Then it runs a long straight reach of bottomland, the Salyer Wildlife Refuge, all the way to the Manitoba border. North of the border the Souris gathers Antler Creek. I parked the car frequently and walked in over private land to find the river in these places. The Souris finally runs out in the Assiniboine like the flare of a trumpet. The Assiniboine joins the Red River near Winnipeg, and from Lake Winnipeg, in a flow too difficult to trace, the diffused memory of the Souris passes down the Nelson and into Hudson Bay.

I needed a sense of the entire lay of the river in those first two years. But it was in the great bend of the Souris in northern North Dakota, the river we called the Mouse when I was a boy, somewhere in that fifty miles of open country between Salyer Refuge in the east and the Upper Souris Refuge to the west, that I believed what I wanted might be found. I rented a motel room in Sherwood and concentrated my search north of State Highway 256, the road running straight east from Sherwood to Westhope. Each day, from one spot or another, I'd hike the few miles from the road up to the Canadian border. Sometimes I'd camp where I thought the border was and the next day walk back to the truck. What I was alert for was a bird's cry, a pattern of purple and yellow flowers in a patch of needlegrass, the glint of a dragonfly—a turn of emotion that would alter my sense of alignment.

In the spring of 1994, walking a dry stretch of upper Cut Bank Creek, I came on the tracks of three or four unshod horses. I followed the short trail out of prairie grass onto fine silt in the river bed, where it then turned abruptly back onto prairie grass and became undetectable. I tested the rim of the hoofprints with my fingertips. I marked the way the horses' hooves had clipped small stones and sent them shooting sideways. In several places the tracks nicked the ground deeply enough to suggest the horses had been carrying riders.

It was hard for me to get away a second time that year. It wasn't until September that I was able to complete and deliver promised work, and when I finally drove north it was with complicating thoughts. Doreen had proposed, and I had enthusiastically accepted. The home we'd made in Ashland suited both of us, and for a while that summer the undertow that had pulled me north went slack. I felt satisfied. It often happens in life, I knew, that while you're searching ardently in one place, the very thing you want turns up in another, and I thought this was what had occurred. But Doreen said I should go on with it. She saw our time spread out still as moonlight on the prairie. She didn't see time being lost to us. She had a deliberateness of movement about her, a steady expression, that led me to consider things slowly.

So that fall—anticipating a familiar motel room and the stark diner in Sherwood—I went back, in a state of wonder at the new arrangement of my life. And I was thinking about the hoofprints. Some of the land north of 256 lies fallow, and Canada's border, like the sight of a distant fence with no gate, turns travelers away here to the west and east toward manned border crossings. The international boundary tends to maintain an outback, a deserted plain on which one traveler might expect to find no trace of another.

I arrived in Sherwood on September 16. With the help of an acquaintance I rented a horse and trailer to let me explore more quickly and extensively along the upper reaches of Cut Bank Creek. On the morning of the seventeenth I parked the truck off the side of the road a few miles east of town and rode north on the mare, a spirited blue roan. I found no fresh horse tracks along the creek bed. Somewhere near the border I turned east. I'd forgotten how much being astride a horse freed the eye. It is the horse, then, that must watch the ground. I'd ridden horses since I was a child, but not recently. I recalled with growing pleasure the way a good horse can measure off a prairie, glide you over its swells.

I was certain I'd walked across parts of this same landscape earlier, but it seemed different to me now, the result of being up on the horse, I thought, and taking in more of a place at a glance than I would on foot. Or it may have been that with the horse under me, traveling seemed less arduous, less distracting. I was watering the mare at a pothole, one of many scattered over these grass plains, when another rider rose up from a swale astride a brown pinto. He did not at first see me. I had a chance to steady myself before our eyes met. The blue roan raised her head from the water but gave no sign of alarm. At her movement the other horse crow-hopped sideways. It took me a moment to separate horse and rider. The pinto bore yellow bars on both forelegs. A trail of red hoofprints ran over its left shoulder, and two feathers spiraled in its mane. The man's dark legs were similarly barred, and there were white dots like hail across his chest. Above a sky-blue neck his chin and mouth were painted black. The upper right half of his face was white. From the left cheek, a bright blue serpentine line rose through his eye and entered his hair. The hair cascaded over his horse's rump, its gleaming black lines spilling to both sides. The man held a simple jaw-loop rein lightly in his left hand. In his right he held out a short bow and an unnocked arrow.

The bold division of his face made its contours hard to read, but the forehead was high, the nose and middle of the face long, his lips full. The adornment of horse and rider blazed against the dun-colored prairie. A halo of intensity surrounded them both, as if they were about to explode. I could read no expression in either face—not fear, not curiosity, not aggression, not even wonder. The man's lips were slightly pursed, suggesting concentration, possibly amusement, as if he had encountered an unexpected test, a stunt meant to throw him.

Of the four of us, only my horse shifted. As she did so, the polished chrome of her bit and the silver conchas on her bridle played sunlight over the other horse and rider. The man's first movement of distraction was to follow the streaks and discs of light running like water across his thighs.

In that moment I remembered enough from a studious childhood to guess the man might be Assiniboin. In the eighteenth century Assiniboin people lived here between the upper Saskatchewan and Missouri Rivers. He could be Cree. He looked half my age.

I turned my reins once around the pommel of the saddle and showed my empty hands, palms out, at my sides.

"My name is Adrian Whippet," I said. "I am only passing through here."

Nothing in his demeanor changed. I'd never seen a human being so alert. He slowly pursed his lips in a more pronounced way, but the trace of amusement was gone. Just then I smelled the other horses, which I turned to see. Another man, his face cut diagonally into triangles of bright red and blue, sat a sorrel mare behind me. He led three horses on a braided rope—a pale dun horse with a black tail and mane carrying pack bags, a black pinto, and a bay with a face stripe. Their flaring nostrils searched the air, their eyes rolled as they took it all in. The second man wore a plain breechclout, like the first. He held no weapon, but studied me as if I were something he was going to hunt.

In a gesture made in response and without thinking, I raised my right arm to point beyond him across the prairie, as though I had something to show or was indicating where we were all headed. I turned the blue roan firmly and started in that direction. It was the direction in which my truck lay and seemed, too, the direction they were traveling. The skin beneath my shirt prickled as I passed before the second man, a chill of sweat. They drew up quickly on each side of me. I was surrounded by the odor of men and horses.

We rode easily together. From time to time they spoke to one another, brief exchanges, unanswered statements. I said nothing. The second man, about the same age as his companion, was leaner. His hair was cut off at the shoulders and raised in a clay-stiffened wall above his forehead. He wore ear pendants of iridescent shell. Wolf tails swung from the heels of his moccasins. I didn't want to stare, but maneuvered my horse in such a way as to fall slightly behind occasionally so I could look more closely at them. From the number of things they carried, skin bundles and parfleches, I guessed they were coming back from a long trip. That would explain the extra horses. Or perhaps they'd been somewhere and stolen the horses.

They, too, tried not to stare, but I sensed them scrutinizing every article of my tack and clothing, every accoutrement. I thought to signal them that we might trade horses, or to demonstrate for them the effect of my sunglasses on the glare coming from the side oats and blue grama grass. But, just as quickly, I let the ideas go. I felt it best to give in to the riding, to carry on with calmness and authority.

Eventually, we stopped glancing at one another and gazed over the country more, studying individual parts of it. In a movement so fast it was finished before I grasped it, the first man shot a large jackrabbit, which he leaned down to snatch from the grass without dismounting. He gutted it with a small sharp tool and spilled the intestines out as we rode along. His movements were as deft as a weaver's, and I felt an unexpected pleasure watching him. He returned my look of admiration with what seemed a self-conscious smile. The harsh afternoon light silvered in a sheen on the horses' necks and flanks, and I heard the flick of their hooves in the cordgrass and bluestem when we crossed damp swales. Hairy seeds of milkweed proceeded so slowly through the air that we passed them by. More often than I, the two men turned to look behind them.

I knew these people no better than two deer I might have stumbled upon, but I was comfortable with them, and the way we fit against the prairie satisfied me. I felt I could ride a very long way like this, absorbed by whatever it was we now shared, a kind of residency. It seemed, because of the absence of fences or the intercession of the horses, or perhaps only as an accident of conducive weather, that we were traveling a seam together. There was nothing to do but ride on, marking the country in unison and feeling the inspiritedness of the afternoon, smelling the leather, the horses, the prairie.

When we came to what I recognized as the intermittently dry bed of Cut Bank Creek, I said the words out loud, "Cut Bank Creek."

The second man said something softly. The first man repeated his words so I could hear, *"Akip atashetwah."*

I lifted my left hand to suggest, again, our trail. First Man mimicked the gesture perfectly, indicating they meant to go in a different direction from mine, north and west. We regarded each other with savor, pleased and wondering but not puzzled. I laid my reins around the pommel and pulled off the belt my father had given me as a wedding present years ago. I cut two of its seventeen sand-cast silver conchas free with a pocketknife. Dismounting, I handed one to each man. Second Man pulled a thin white object from a bag tied to his saddle frame. When he held it out for me, I recognized it as a large bird's wing bone, drilled with a line of small holes. A flute. I remounted with it as First Man stepped to the ground. He lifted a snowy owl feather he'd taken from his horse's mane and tied it into the blue roan's mane.

We rode away without speaking. The first time I looked back, I couldn't see them. I sat the horse and watched the emptiness where they should have been until dusk laid blue and then purple across the grass.

The Deaf Girl

The girl's problem appeared to be deafness, but deafness was
only a pivot around which part of her psyche turned and an
easy thing to notice. Once, standing on the porch of the hotel,
I watched her move through a field of high grass below an
abandoned pear orchard a half mile distant. It was a bright
day in November and the grass was turning saffron and
magenta in the sweep of the wind. She moved in such a tenta-
tive way down the hillside I thought her sightless. But I knew
her to be the deaf girl from this place, and so imagined it was
only how she examined the world that made her appear blind.

She was twelve, the lone child of parents who projected
austerity on the street, one of perhaps eight or nine children
around the town. Occasionally I saw her playing with another
girl, older by a few years, but most often when I saw her she
was walking alone. Her parents called out after her, "Dela-

mina," but the name came to her in some other way, a vibration passing through her body, and she would turn. Closer in, she read the muscles moving in a speaker's face.

I didn't arrive in the town by accident, exactly, but initially it was not my intention even to stop. I drove out of Great Falls on the Missouri before dawn, late July, and headed for Williston in North Dakota. At Lewiston I turned north on the road for Malta. I'd crossed the river, and somewhere south of the Fort Belknap Reservation I turned east on a state road I thought would shorten the distance to Glasgow. North of the Fort Peck Reservoir, in a series of crests and troughs, the cottonwood draws and their bare hills, I became confused. After an hour of just pushing on regardless, I drove in to what I thought was Telegraph Creek, but it wasn't, it was Gannett. A few storefronts and houses on its main street, a few stand-alone buildings, and a scatter of mobile homes at the end of dirt tracks splayed like tendrils away from the road, which ended here.

An old-fashioned two-story hotel, the Essex, stood in good repair and it was suppertime so I went in to eat, and then took a room when I learned from the clerk where I was, and where I had to go to get back on the road for Glasgow and U.S. 2 on in to Williston.

The town was an oddity in eastern Montana. Barely a sign of ranching and none of mining. No railroad. No Indian faces. It was agreeable country, the short-grass prairie appealing with its seasonal creeks and woody draws. It might have been homesteaded early on, but the sign of constancy in it was its flocks of crows calling, the pale sky and the short grama grass.

The meal was good and well served, the room comfortable, without a phone or television, without advertising or promotional circulars. The mood in the hotel was akin to that at some resorts, each thing perfectly tended to but the overall atmosphere undisturbed. Any inchoate threat of retaliation one might have experienced, or the weight of indifference known from moments lived out in airports and buildings among strangers, was absent here. I opened the sash-weighted windows and abandoned myself to a deep and dreamless sleep.

My obligations in Williston, attending to some details of my father's will, were not pressing. I remained in Gannett for three days.

The single store in town, a kind of mercantile, had much to covet in the way of antiques—old carpenter's tools, some well-preserved harness, equipment I recognized for candle-making, and about fifty running feet of old paperbacks. The first morning I went through the books title by title and bought two, but when I stepped outside again I realized that was where I wanted to be, out, on foot and looking up north past the orchard where the road didn't go, where the land dipped into a swale and then rose into low curving hills and fell away again. If, in fact, it hadn't been farmed it could have been for stones in the soil, some rock like flint that tore the plows apart. Standing in the street that morning I saw her for the first time, walking in from the hills and up to a white house with dark green trim, which she entered.

Who can say why a person or a place is attractive? I found Gannett and the hotel and the cant of the girl's stride to be so, and stayed on the extra days to know why. I read one of the paperbacks on the hotel porch, hoping the why of it would come over me, but it didn't. A few people passed in and out of the store. Someone drove away south out of town. In the afternoon, I watched five children at play. They might have spent the morning in class together in someone's home. Remembering those days now, it occurs to me that outside of ordinary noises—a door closing, an engine starting, the ticking of wood cooling in the hotel's walls in the night—one sound hummed beneath it all, the streaming down of light from the empty sky.

I drove off early that last day and went on to Williston. It was a year before I returned, backtracking the roads from Glasgow. I had no other idea but to eat at the hotel and read. It was on that trip that I saw the girl wading through the waist-high grass in her black frock, like another sort of bare-limbed, rain-darkened tree, a cogitating body. The clerk at the Essex told me she'd lost her hearing in a shooting accident, but I guessed there was more than this and let our conversation go into awkward silences until he gave me the rest, that she'd been hit in the head by a stray bullet one night in Long Beach, that it had eclipsed the hearing in both ears, and the day she got out of the hospital her father moved them, straight to northeastern Montana from south L.A. The same day I saw her crossing the hillside, I passed her on the street. Her blue eyes were fierce as black jet; the determination in her face approached a leer. She didn't even glance toward me.

The first time I returned to Gannett—and I came back only once after that—I was having an evening cigar on the hotel porch after a day of wind and rain, and in that baleful light I spotted a figure walking in from the north, a boy with a rifle balanced across his shoulder, the barrel forward in his fist. I could tell it was a boy by the stride. As he came on I saw his silhouetted head was close-cropped and that his jeans bagged in a style popular in large cities but rarely seen at the time in rural Montana. A dog followed which looked pensive and dour and mostly bluetick hound.

The boy chucked his chin as he went by, but in a surly manner. The dog glanced up as he passed, but with no more interest than if he were taking in the familiar chair, occasionally occupied.

I smoked the cigar out, ate supper, and retired. I was reading a collection of unsettling stories I'd bought called *Jesus' Son*. Its premises kept me awake until two, after which I decided to get up and go down to the porch and sit in the moonlight. A flaring match to light another cigar would have ruined the stillness, quite inseparable from the moonlight, so I only sat there in a jacket and my undershorts. I was not surprised when I saw a small figure walking the same path the boy had walked hours before. It was a continuation of a disturbance, one initiated by the boy's passing, and it was this that had really brought me out onto the porch. I soon saw that it was the girl, and I could tell that it was bad, the lopsided way that she advanced, sweeping a hand in front of her to locate obstruction. I sat rigid, a motionless spectator.

I could pick out little detail in the dimness, but when she drew near I saw plainly the dark welt of blood congealed like paint on her face and run out across her chest in her blouse. I didn't want to move my eyes, to deliberately examine her body, but I sensed her clothing was twisted, and one hand hung still and distorted. He had left her for dead, I thought.

She stopped a few feet away. Her disheveled body seemed an object dragged in the wake of her will.

"Are you all right?" I asked. Despite her wounds she appeared calm, even invulnerable.

"He's got a surprise," she said evenly. Within the keep of herself, I imagined, she had not heard my question. "He knows I was shot before," she continued. "He wanted to be part of that. He was always asking to see the wound. The thought of it, the bullet going through my head, made him excited. He wanted to see where it went in, where it came out, and put his fingers against the places. And then he did it himself, shot me in the head. He pulled down my pants. And then he walked away. But I'm here now and he has to look at me. He has to look right here"—she lifted the stiff hand to her creased temple—"where the bullet went, be forced to look at it until he makes a mess in his pants. For him, that's going to be the beginning."

I wanted to stop her, cut her off. I didn't know where the boy lived, where a doctor might be, and, strangely, had no urge to help. The girl was eerie in her stillness and independence. She'd suffered adversity, and perhaps knew better than I now what she needed to hold herself together. The boy would suffer. I knew there was hell to pay for this, and for the other shooting.

She had me fixed with a stare from her dark face. Her breath was winded but steady. It seemed she expected me to go with her.

I stood up, gesturing at my legs. "I haven't got any pants on here. I've got to get my pants." I lit a wooden match and held it to my lips. "Where's the boy? Where's he live?"

She remained still as a dog with a leg shot away.

I guessed the boy might be sleeping in a trailer somewhere, maybe with the gun. What about her parents, why weren't they out looking? Why weren't people off searching, lights on, the sheriff arriving? Nothing but the girl alone.

"You can't take his life," I continued. I struck another match. "You can't hurt him back for what he did, can't kill him for it, even if it's justified. Only the state can kill him," I counseled. "If it's premeditated, if he left you for dead, then the state will do that."

She drew in a breath through clenched teeth. I could tell from the angle of her head, the flick of her good hand, that she was done. What did she want from me? How could this be business of mine? She stepped back and turned to cross the street, walking toward two buildings and a path between them that led to a trailer house.

I whiffed the match out. I watched her enter, halt but straight, the building's shadows. I loped the opposite way, across the street toward her house. Maybe someone there would help. I couldn't; nor could I help the boy. She was out there somewhere, way past where I had gone. She was walking in from some distant place, and I knew I had to get there.

Rubén Mendoza Vega, Suzuki Professor of Early Caribbean History, University of Florida at Gainesville, Offers a History of the United States Based on Personal Experience

In 1524,[1] an ancestor of my father[2] named Bernardo Marín[3] received a land grant[4] from Hernán Cortés.[5] He expanded these holdings until in the seventh generation[6] the family controlled[7] an extent of tobacco[8] fields unexcelled in the New World.[9] My son, with no grasp of history,[10] no sense of proportion about the broad effects of tobacco,[11] and a Romanticist's infatuation with the Indian,[12] repudiated his heritage in an act of suicide. When Communism fails in Cuba, as it must, and Castro[13] flees, our family will again take up its place on the island.[14] We will once again make the finest cigars in the world. And I will resist feelings of bitterness toward a middle son[15] who could not wait. His grandfather told him as I did: patience. In this neglected virtue[16] is the story of America.

NOTES

1. As a historian I have an obligation in my short paper to the exigencies and dictates of my profession, as well as a duty of courtesy toward the reader. I must, therefore, make clear at the outset that even though I am dealing for the most part with primary materials in the archives of my own family, I have after many years of meticulous research and also careful comparison with contemporaneous histories developed the confidence to let my family stand, like Everyman, for all families. (And I now provide access to these documents, formally, to my fellow historians.) I must state, too, that in my paper, which deals with incidents familiar even in their detail to amateur historians, I have deliberately chosen to consult not just lesser-known works, or works not as yet translated into the major research languages, but works that are at odds with contemporary historical thought. In doing so, I realize I open myself to criticism and invite contempt for the foundation of my ideas. But how else a fresh wind?

2. Julio Cartena Mejordigas. My family dropped in 1912 the Spanish practice of a doubled surname, commemorating the lineages of both parents. Wilford F. Grace, in the closing years of a brilliant career at the University of Witwatersrand, devoted himself to the study of my father's correspondence with relatives in Asturias. My father, a manic-depressive personality, wrote obsessively to even remote relatives in a kind of pathetic (though to me quite noble) attempt to clarify his place in history. It was he, for all his good points, who first gave my middle son, Petrero, whose life I take up at the end of my essay, doubts about his lineage. See "Julio Cartena Mejordigas: The Early Correspondence (1936–43)" by W. F. Grace in *South African Review of Colonial History* 18, no. 4 (1967): 54–78; and *The Asturian Temperament* by Nolan I. Benito.

3. In addition to material in the family archives at the University

of Texas at Austin, the reader is directed to the Marín Collection at the municipal library in Santander and to the Cormuello Collection of Cuban Historical Documents at the University of Oviedo. Marín was a sailmaker and an innovator of stitching techniques as well as the developer of a resinous treatment for sail thread that made early sixteenth-century Spanish sails, with their greater flexibility in cold weather and resistance to rot, the envy of European mariners. See *The Advent of European Power* by Hu-Li Huang; *Galician Sailcraft* by George G. Borcello; and " 'El Hilo Maravilloso': A Key to Early Sixteenth-Century Spanish Sea Power" by M.D.R. Meltwater in *Atlantic Maritime History* 108, no. 5 (1974): 435–88.

Marín sailed with Cortés and is mentioned in the standard biographies in his capacity as sailmaker-to-the-fleet; but references are few to his agrarian predilections and to his more or less sudden shift of occupation, which occurred when he was granted 17.6 hectares of arable land and the services of 30 indigenous workers in Cuba. I have been in correspondence with Roberta Nesserman-Phillips of the Department of History at Florida International University, who is preparing a book-length manuscript of Marín's early years in Cuba, including his role in the suppression of the Mortemos Revolt. Early drafts of her manuscript make it plain that the renowned sailmaker and the lesser-known agrarian pioneer are one and the same, a point contested some years ago by Makelos Kostermela in a seminal article, "Technical Achievement in Sixteenth-Century French, English, and Spanish Sailcraft," in *Journal of Sewn and Fastened Materials* 16, no. 7 (1947): 136–59. See also "Early Agrarian Reform Movements in the Caribbean" by Victor Brent in *Panamanian Perspectives* 44, no. 2 (1985): 227–89; and *L'Insurrection des indigènes de l'île de Cuba et la répression espagnole* by Jean-Bédel Bosschère, pp. 508–15.

4. The property, a grant from Carlos V made upon the recom-

mendation of Cortés, was one of sixteen Cortés authorized in 1524, each of equal size, the so-called "peach," or "durazno," of 17.6 hectares (43.5 acres). The grant was located in the southern piedmont of the Organos Mountains in the Pinar del Río, at the heart of what was to become the Vuelta Abajo. At this time the land was not so highly valued that Marín could not purchase tracts cheaply and trade to his advantage, perhaps with a sense of intuition. At the time of his death in 1551, he held title to 251 hectares (620.2 acres).

The land-grant system of patronage in early Cuban history was, of course, politically motivated, and the process was subject to a certain amount of corruption. One must be careful, however, not to assume unblessed intentions prevailed or that invidious plots existed where none has been proven. Among the most lucid and penetrating analyses of this volatile aspect of Spanish colonial history is "Terrenos en barbecho, trabajadores disponibles: Una visión de agricultura duradera," a 1988 doctoral dissertation by Manuel Peña, which draws heavily on two obscure works: *La punizione di Cuba* by Luigi Pernotti and *Servitus in Novo Mundo* by Henri Latrousse, S.J.

5. Cortés, of course, has been studied handily by Demott, Esperanza, Bouchald, Clackas, Merriman, and Dorger. All of these biographies are rich and each one is distinctly valuable. Among more recent work, both the Tesraffe and Urbanowitz biographies suffer in my mind from vindictiveness and offer no improvement on earlier scholarship. Quite the contrary is true of *Cortés and the Institution of an Imperial Order* by Esther Manas vanKamp. She not only brings to bear her extensive knowledge of the Tomás de Bivar collection, which has only recently been opened to scholars, but pioneers a psychoanalytic approach long missing in studies of Cortés. In addition to her singular modern work, see her "Iconography in the Mexican Journals of Cortés" in *Journal of Historical Psychoanalysis* 52, no. 3 (1989): 279–301.

6. In tracing the lineage of fifty-one New World families of Spanish origin whose founders arrived in the Caribbean in the sixteenth century, I've found that with thirty-six the consolidation of great wealth came in the seventh generation. (By great wealth I mean a perennial wealth, an aggregation of investment, credit, and land that cannot be depleted at that point by scandal, squandering of opportunity, ordinary prodigality, or even criminal activity.) I am no mathematician; but, noting that this wealth does inexplicably begin to dissipate in the eighth generation and that by the ninth or tenth generation, it is on a par with that, respectively, of the fifth and fourth generations, a formula is present here seemingly worth divining.

7. A relative term, which benefits from the clarification offered in Carlson Kildfray's *Subterranean Economics*. Kildfray has, of course, been heavily criticized for his putative insensitivity to human plight; but I believe he comes closer in his work to sixteenth- and seventeenth-century economic reality in the Spanish Caribbean than any other economic historian. The fact is that Taino, Ciboney, Cuna, Island Carib, Mosquito, and other indigenes were at a primary level of social and economic organization, but this was not their fault. It was necessary that they be brought along quickly with the development of New World wealth; and it was inevitable in such a process that some individuals would be treated roughly. In *El florecimiento de la economía política occidental* by Juan Ramón Aruba and Kasumasa Asahi's *Dotchakuteki keizai chitsujo no jokyo* (The elimination of indigenous economic boundaries), such provocative concepts as "ordained wealth," "penetration economics," and "disparity compassion" are subjected to stunning exegeses.

The storm-tossed subject of the exercise of economic and political control in previously occupied New World territories having been addressed, the further question of authority in these new lands vis-à-vis the desires of competing colonial family groups arises; and here, certainly, we have some dark chapters before us. For a discussion of criminal subterfuge among the ruling classes in the Spanish Caribbean, see *Politika potrebleniia i politicheskii konflikt v Kube xvii veka* (Consummation policies and political conflict in seventeenth-century Cuba) by Maldano Pestrovich. For a frank discussion of extortion and murder among the same, see "The Tenebrous Light of Grief: The Economy of Santo Domingo and Cuba in the Sixteenth Century" by Beverly Weissbaum in *International Journal of Colonial Theory* 62, no. 2 (1986): 1245–91.

Alternative views of indigenous land rights, and the legal and moral implications arising therefrom, are ably set out in Malcolm Batson's *A Woeful Tide* and *Créatures de la lune* by Rebecca Tide Assiminy.

8. Although a strong home market for tobacco developed almost immediately after colonization by the Spanish, the cultivation of tobacco in Cuba did not begin until 1580, according to Demster Poltcaza in his authoritative *Tobacco: Its Origin and Production*. Bernardo Marín, however, in a letter to his father dated 15 May 1545 (BMLS 3.4506), states that he seeded his first crop of *Nicotiana tabacum* in the spring of that year. As nearly as I can determine, he was the first to export Cuban tobacco, probably by 1548.

In another letter to his father, dated 22 August 1548 (BMLS 3.4811), Marín sets forth the reasons for planting this crop and speculates about his success. He makes reference to several precipitating dreams and, of course, to the vagaries of Spanish colonial shipping. The most astonishing line in this letter is his contention that "the proceeds [from the tobacco crop] will ensure the wealth of my descendants in these wretched and primitive lands to the seventh generation."

The contributions of his descendants to the development of tobacco varieties are substantial (cf. *Tobacco Leaf: Its Culture and*

Cure by T. E. Roberson, pp. 257–61); and the fame of the family's cigar leaf, unsurpassed for aroma, was widespread by the end of the seventeenth century. Oddly, Marín himself did not smoke. As well as I can determine, García Mendoza, in the fourth generation (b. 1643), was the first member of the family to smoke. Tobacco cultivation was first and foremost a business, in the establishment and development of which Bernardo Marín and his descendants were very aggressive.

9. A statement hard to defend, certainly, but so crucial to my theme that I have felt justified in the extraordinarily time-consuming work needed to justify it. With the help of several assistants, whose labors I hereby gratefully acknowledge, I reviewed the holdings of all the tobacco-growing families in the Caribbean and in the North American colonies in 1735, when the firstborn son in the seventh generation married. The patriarch of the family in that year, Diego Marín Tréllez, owned 2,114 hectares (5,223.7 acres); his two brothers controlled between them another 728 hectares (1,798.9 acres). The total, 2,842 hectares (7,022.6 acres) devoted exclusively to the cultivation of tobacco, exceeds by 188 hectares (464.5 acres) the holdings of the Carlos family of Santo Domingo, the next highest total. For reference, the largest holdings in the North American colonies in 1735, those of the Benson family in Virginia, totaled only 403 hectares (995.8 acres).

10. Although well educated at Hotchkiss and Yale, and holding graduate degrees in economics from Stanford and in political science from the University of Texas at Austin, my son disparaged history as a discipline (possibly a reaction to his father's profession, therefore not a true denial). In the closing years of his life, he spoke incessantly of "revisionist histories," by which he meant any history, no matter how pathetic or meager its scholarship, that condescended to ideas of progress or that was critical of the civilizing influence of the colonizing nations in the New World. He took a

perverse pleasure, I believe, in actually funding some of the more irresponsible and insipid of these publications, which do not merit cataloging here. His grasp of history, the general flow of events, I believe was exceptional; but his failure to perceive the concatenation that gives history its intellectual tension and its meaning, his blindness to the filaments of cause, were almost complete by the last year of his life. The despair that reliably follows on the abandonment of any original wisdom no doubt contributed to his wayward behavior and the sense of futility that overcame his sense of hope.

I would hasten to add in his defense that he was no supporter of Castro.

11. No gift of the New World, with the possible exception of gold, brought with it a more salubrious effect than tobacco. In the contemporary political climate, where health issues are confounded by a politics of righteousness and intimidation, it is helpful to recall that for hundreds of years the cultivation of tobacco, the manufacture of tobacco products, and tobacco's sale and distribution were a source of the deepest kind of agrarian pleasure, of fundamental dignity in the workplace, and of material wealth for hundreds of thousands of people. Conflicting scientific evidence indicates that nicotine, tarry compounds, and carbon monoxide from cigar and cigarette smoking *may* affect *some* individuals adversely, but a far greater number of tobacco users very likely suffer no ill effects. Indeed, were it not for the contentious political climate surrounding the cultivation and marketing of this plant, the pleasures it offers might be extolled as are the pleasures of wine, the varieties of cheese, or the benefits of any other of nature's products not (yet) subject to vehement attack—in which, one might justifiably add, an opposition to capitalism is transparently clear.

12. The literature here, of course, is voluminous. For my pur-

poses I have been interested principally in publications of historians and other scholars on the "second war," the second round of negotiations with indigenes in the New World, largely diplomatic, to settle "land claims" and allied issues of political geography. Again, while the literature in defense of these claims, from both the scholarly and legal quarters, is in its ascendency, the countervailing thought of those who see the grave dangers posed to stable economies by the pursuit of such claims is in dire need of review. *The Distant Shore* by Muriel Cagney, Estone Bazzergahnah's *The Triple Alliance: Environment, Indians, and Pacifists,* and *Les faux dieux: Échec de l'ecuménisme* by Etienne Crochet are early, praiseworthy attempts to separate *nihil ad rem* anthropological thinking from what is, at base, really only an economic debate.

The profusion of popular pro-indigene writing need not concern us here; scholarly writing in this vein is still largely self-defeating because of its polemical tone and tendentious structure. Nevertheless, several recent works, one must say assiduously researched and presented in an evenhanded way, deserve careful reading: among them are *Killing the Horses, Scattering the Sheep* by Adrian Nightwalker; *Iktome Reality* by Thomas Yellow Calf; and Harrison Wood's *Bears Fall from the Sky.* All, of course, are inimical to Western civilization.

13. The surprising durability and resilience of the Castro regime are the subject of three new works: *Los consejos militares de la Sierra Occidental* by José Mellín; *Die Entstehung eines PolizeiStaats in Castros Kuba* by Ladislaw Krupp; and *The Betrayal of Cuban Dreams* by Aktannis Moulifiz. A new dual biography of Ernesto Guevara and Juan Perón, *Guevara and Perón* by Percy St. Evrain, takes advantage of recently discovered papers in the archives of the University of Buenos Aires to clarify Guevara's role in the twenty-sixth of July movement. In his closing chapter, St. Evrain offers an original analysis of Castro's demagoguery.

14. At the Institute of Land Registry in Miami, work on recording and verifying the holdings of displaced Cuban families is now virtually complete. When these families are permitted to return to Cuba, they will take up the daunting but ultimately gratifying task of restoring the Cuban economy. The shattering experience of being driven from lands productively and continuously occupied, in some cases for more than four hundred years, will be over. The Indian psychologist and political scientist Nadali Misra, almost in anticipation of these events, has written a most pertinent essay, "The Healing Effect of Reclamation in Birth-Right Land Disputes" in *Journal of Oceanian Psychology* 24, no. 6 (1991): 402–28.

15. Relevant issues of primogeniture are taken up in Furman Bodfield's *The Fate of the Second Son,* pp. 206–35, 288–89, 310–12, and 416–24. The related issue of parental disappointment in offspring is addressed in Simon Bednar's *Suspended Gratification.*

I am preparing my son's journals for publication, partly in the hope that a pattern of development in his revisionist thinking will emerge and that it will be seen to comprise part of a larger intellectual problem in his generation: a general denial of the good.

16. In the modern era, with its jaded observations and typically cynical analysis of the human effort to ensure a rewarding life, it is challenging to convene an amicable forum for the discussion of simple virtue. Yet without virtuous behavior, every society unravels (see *La degradación de la esperanza* by Philip Llosa). To succeed in life, to post a record of tenacity, thrift, shrewdness, and courage, such as that which distinguishes the descendants of Bernardo Marín, requires the studied application of virtue. Without it there is no wealth, no leisure, no triumph. In his brilliant critical biography of De Gaulle, Emilion Klugge-Wrasse contends that if a leader is without virtue, those whom he leads will fail to comprehend their destiny; but a virtuous leader will inspire a nation with what is right in all spheres of activity, from aesthetic to economic.

In America, the role of virtuous achievement is so deeply embedded in the culture it can even transcend poor leadership. In *Casting a Cloak Before the Sun*, Cándido Argüello writes that in America it is impossible to understand either business or politics without reference to the desire to lead a virtuous life. This is a daring statement, worthy of careful review.

BIBLIOGRAPHY

Argüello, Cándido. *Casting a Cloak Before the Sun*. Houston: Arte Público, 1989.

Aruba, Juan Ramón. *El florecimiento de la economía política occidental*. Madrid: Planeta, 1980.

Asahi, Kasumasa. *Dotchakuteki keizai chitsujo no jokyo* [The elimination of indigenous economic boundaries]. Tokyo: Kodansha, 1982.

Assiminy, Rebecca Tide. *Créatures de la lune*. Paris: Lumière Blanche, 1985.

Batson, Malcolm. *A Woeful Tide*. London: Faber & Faber, 1984.

Bazzergahnah, Estone. *The Triple Alliance: Environment, Indians, and Pacifists*. Columbus, Oh.: Merrill, 1981.

Bednar, Simon. *Suspended Gratification*. New York: New York University Press, 1965.

Benito, Nolan I. *The Asturian Temperament*. Austin: University of Texas Press, 1964.

Bodfield, Furman. *The Fate of the Second Son*. New York: Praeger, 1987.

Borcello, George G. *Galician Sailcraft*. Annapolis: Naval Institute Press, 1967.

Bosschère, Jean-Bédel. *L'Insurrection des indigènes de l'île de Cuba et la répression espagnole*. Paris: Seuil, 1975.

Bouchald, Guillaume. *Libérateur des Antilles*. Paris: Masson, 1973.

Cagney, Muriel. *The Distant Shore.* Oxford: Oxford University Press, 1983.

Clackas, Miriam. *The Vision of Cortés.* Nedlands, Western Australia: University of Western Australia Press, 1983.

Crochet, Etienne. *Les faux dieux: Échec de l'ecuménisme.* Paris: Gauthier, 1986.

Demott, Arthur. *The Rise of Cortés.* Oxford: Pergamon, 1967.

Dorger, Heinrich. *Cortés: Die Kuba-Jahre.* Berlin: Altberliner, 1981.

Esperanza, Julio. *Hernán Cortés: Creador de la identidad americana.* Barcelona: Scriba, 1956.

Huang, Hu-Li. *The Advent of European Power.* Baltimore: The Johns Hopkins University Press, 1973.

Kildfray, Carlson. *Subterranean Economics.* Chicago: University of Chicago Press, 1979.

Klugge-Wrasse, Emilion. *De Gaulle et l'Europe d'après-guerre.* Lyon: Meridien, 1962.

Krupp, Ladislaw. *Die Entstehung eines Polizei-Staats in Castros Kuba.* München: Strauss, 1972.

Latrousse, S.J., Henri. *Servitus in Novo Mundo.* Vatican City: Biblioteca Apostolica Vaticana, 1888.

Llosa, Philip. *La degradación de la esperanza.* Barcelona: Muñoz, 1989.

Mellín, José. *Los consejos militares de la Sierra Occidental.* Mexico City: Campeador, 1975.

Merriman, Wendell. *The Policies of Cortés.* Cape Town: Codding & Vandermeer, 1959.

Moulifiz, Aktannis. *The Betrayal of Cuban Dreams.* London: Stokes, 1968.

Nightwalker, Adrian. *Killing the Horses, Scattering the Sheep.* Chinle, Arizona: Navajo Community College Press, 1991.

Peña, Manuel. "Terrenos en barbecho, trabajadores disponibles: Una visión de agricultura duradera." Ph.D. diss., Southern Methodist University, 1988.

Pernotti, Luigi. *La punizione di Cuba*. Milano: Milano Libri, 1926.

Pestrovich, Maldano. *Politika potrebleniia i politicheskii konflikt v Kube xvii veka* [Consummation policies and political conflict in seventeenth-century Cuba]. Moscow: Politizdat, 1932.

Poltcaza, Demster. *Tobacco: Its Origin and Production*. New York: Doubleday, 1954.

Roberson, T. E. *Tobacco Leaf: Its Culture and Cure*. Washington: Institute for Tobacco Research, 1957.

St. Evrain, Percy. *Guevara and Perón*. London: Macmillan, 1990.

Tesraffe, Miguel. *La caída de México*. Mexico City: Ediciones Xochiti, 1984.

Urbanowitz, Grigorii. *Politicheskie namereniia Ispanii v Meksike* [Spain's designs in Mexico]. Leningrad: Nauka, 1985.

vanKamp, Esther Manas. *Cortés and the Institution of an Imperial Order*. Montreal: Pontes, 1987.

Wood, Harrison. *Bears Fall from the Sky*. Minneapolis: Graywolf Press, 1984.

Yellow Calf, Thomas. *Iktome Reality*. New York: Knopf, 1990.

The Letters of Heaven

When I was a boy of thirteen I found a packet of letters in my father's desk. I picked the lock to the drawer one day with one of my mother's hairpins. Then, to keep my curiosity from being discovered, I took the small desk key one time when my father was sick, and in a distant quarter of Lima I had a stranger make a copy. That way I didn't run the risk, each time I opened the drawer, of mutilating the lock and having my sin exposed.

The letters had been written in Castilian Spanish in the first decade of the seventeenth century between a man and a woman who did not sign their names but who wrote in exquisite phrases of desire and anguish about their passion for each other. During the years I read and reread these letters, I thought them composed of the most beautiful and, at the same time, the most illicit of human statements. The language of enthrallment was so unrestrained that the images existed for me outside the realm of sin and redemption, beyond the sphere of the Church. Please understand the complication— sometimes in reading the words I found myself with a powerful erection, but I did not consider this state of excitement, the vibrating ventilation of my skin, a violation of the sixth or ninth commandment. I felt my longing took place on another plane. I felt that my desire drew on many human emotions, and so was round, perfectly round and full—hunger, weeping, joy, even a peculiar fleeting anger. The shuddering ecstasy I experienced did not produce for me the sign of a sinful act, which I always imagined as quills sprouting suddenly from my face.

Repeated readings would eventually have broken the letters' folds and marred them, so I copied each one out, word for word, and hid the copies in the ceiling of the house. I rarely went afterward to that drawer in my father's desk. When I did, I held what I called the letters of heaven so respectfully my fingers trembled. I wanted desperately to protect a quality in them I understood as purity. I could have memorized them—they were short and there were only nine—but I felt to memorize the letters would have diminished their effect. I was then, too, someone anxious about the lack of substance in memory.

In 1967, when I was eighteen, my father developed cancer. Without health insurance he knew his death was imminent, and so he soon completed the arrangements he wished to make with everyone, loving gestures that put each of us at ease. He spoke with my two uncles, the brothers with whom he ran a tannery, about the disposition of his interest there, including the skiving knives and mallets that had been his father's. He bestowed small gifts on each of his relatives. And through the generosity of his love, by the breadth of his consideration of us, he steered my mother and my sisters and myself toward a rarefied emotional position. It was as though he were tearing himself neatly out of a book while taking pains to see the page would not be missed. Even as he was dying we began to sense that we were whole without him. We would miss him very much, but he was leaving us with a grief that strengthened us.

When it came my turn to have a private moment with my father, he said without warning, "The letters, Ramón, are the most holy, the most beautiful relics in our family. You must protect them. If you have children, give them to the child who is most drawn to them. If you do not, look among your sisters' children for the one who should receive them."

At eighteen I was too old to behave like a child, even before a dying father. I could not openly and fully express the remorse and embarrassment I felt at that moment. I did not know how to beg his forgiveness. I sensed for the first time that my clandestine involvement with the letters had been a sin.

"Who wrote them?" I asked.

"Her name was Isabel, the man was called Martín."

"Were they relatives who came to Peru?"

"Yes. Isabel's brother Fernandino is your ancestor on my father's side, fourteen generations back."

I thought about that name, Fernandino, and I suddenly felt

the quills pressing against the skin of my scalp. "And the man who loved her, Martín—who were his descendants? Are they living here?"

"He did not have any children," my father answered. After a moment he said, "Is this hard for you, Ramón?"

The quills were now out. I wanted to run far away until I disappeared like an ash in the wind. "Is it Rosa de Lima?" I asked. I felt tears of fright.

"Yes," he said, reaching for my hand and holding it. "She was Rosa de Lima, he was Martín de Porres."

I was confounded. "These are the letters of saints!" I blurted.

"They are."

"But how can you—it is blasphemy, it is blasphemous!"

"No, no, Ramón, it is love. It is the love of Christ. My son, you must already know this in your soul."

"I know nothing," I shouted, pulling my hand away, "except that there is a sin here, a terrible sin." I did not want my feelings to overwhelm me, but I could feel the flush of an emotion akin to rage building inexorably with the evidence of this deception.

"There is no sin here, Ramón. I do not even believe your taking my key and making a copy was a sin. You were the person meant to have these letters."

"But what were they doing?" I yelled at him. "What were they doing?"

"Whatever was between them, all my life I have believed it was with God's blessing."

"Please excuse me, Father, but how can you speak like this on your deathbed!"

"Isn't it just now, just in this moment, Ramón, that you have changed your mind about what you have read and thought about for so many years? And yet, what has changed? Nothing. Only that another person knows. It is not the discovery of sin that is filling you with insecurity, Ramón, it is the discovery of the intimacy of real people."

I didn't know what to answer or what to confirm.

"I'm not asking you to share a knowledge of the letters with anyone, not even for you to turn back to them if you cannot bear it. My only request is that you protect them. In each generation they have had a guardian, someone to protect them from the righteous, from those who support the black-and-white distinctions of the Manichaeans, who indulge their hatred of the body. Do you understand?"

"You are saying that I must protect them from the Church?"

"Yes, but not just the Church."

I could not imagine how even to approach this task. I moved to the foot of his bed and sat in a chair.

"Ramón," he implored, "sometimes, after reading the letters, did you touch yourself?"

I could not answer.

"It was the same for me, when I was your age."

"I did not confess what happened to me as a sin," I said after a while.

"I know. I didn't either. This is what I have been trying to make clear. You must not change your feelings now because you know who wrote the letters. Do you see?"

"I will protect them," I answered. I meant it, but it was as close to speaking a lie as it is possible to come.

I burned my copies of the letters in the hour after I left my father's room. Rosa de Lima was Isabel de Flores y Oliva, the first person from the New World to be canonized. Her friend was Martín de Porres, a mulatto canonized three hundred years later. It was not the existence of their love but how to believe in its sanctity that troubled and offended me. I did not want to know how such things could be acceptable for saints.

When my father died I came into possession of the desk with the locked drawer, but I did not look at the correspondence again for more than ten years and then only to move it to another place. Occasionally I would recall a sentence, a paragraph, and it would remain with me for days.

In the summer of 1995 I was working in the library at the University of Lima, researching a paper for a scholarly journal on the early architecture of the city. After my father died, I'd gone to Italy to school, then to France and Barcelona for a while before returning to Lima. I married Camilla, whom I had known first in secondary school, and settled into a comfortable marriage with three children. The quiet domesticity of this life contrasted with my passion for work and certain ideas. I had opened a practice as an architect. My principal interests were the use of local Peruvian stone for building, the survival of Inca techniques for working the stone, and what you would have to call my curiosity about non-Euclidean physics—the development among native workmen of a kind of hybrid structural engineering that derived from alternative ideas about what holds things up. In the case of some of the older buildings in Lima, many of my concerns came together—Quechua masons had raised stone walls buttressed in perfectly sound yet wonderfully unorthodox ways.

Over the years of my professional practice I gravitated steadily toward university teaching. I found it satisfying to support the enthusiasm of younger students, and I was always glad to find one or two who were interested in the things I was interested in. During that summer of 1995 I had two such students working for me, Pedro de Ortega and Analilia Valencia. We were studying some peculiarities in seventeenth-century public buildings in Lima and Callao, when—during the course of our library research—I came upon a second set of letters between Rosa and Martín.

The moment I saw them I was certain that no one else knew what they were. Like the first letters these were unaddressed and unsigned, but the handwriting, the idiosyncrasies in punctuation and grammar, were identical. There were twenty-two of them, on the same color and texture of paper, randomly leaved in a dozen folders of unsorted material within a single box—bills of sale, ships' manifests, and public memoranda— all from the seventeenth century.

The day I discovered the letters I made a thorough search of the only other boxes of unsorted documents on the shelves to satisfy myself there were no others. By then it was after eleven in the evening. I considered concealing the letters and taking them home with me. I had not thought much about Rosa and Martín since that conversation with my father, but here I was again, acting in violation of my principles. I placed the letters in my briefcase and walked out of the library, using my authority as a professor of the university to take advantage.

When I arrived at the house Camilla was already asleep. Our youngest child, Manco, was watching television. I went directly to my study, locked the door, and read each letter carefully. The experience, carrying far into the night, shattered a carapace I had carried unacknowledged for thirty years. These letters were less explicit than the others about sexual ecstasy, but the same overwhelming testimony to the power of the physical body flew up from them. And I could now make a different sense of their meaning. These two people had grown swiftly to accept that ecstatic love was an element of spirituality, that it intensified rather than quenched the light of God. They set forth this belief so boldly it raised the hair on the back of my head.

I sat with the letters until first light, through tears that became fits of weeping, through moments of regret, of terror and resolve, reading again and again sentences in which one or the other recognized the immanence of God in the moisture of rose petals crushed between them or in a burst of wind that entwined their hair. I sat in a state of wonder at their humanity, the fearless, complete acceptance of passion. I trembled as an observer reading at the edge of this embrace, for centuries condemned. What for some couples would have been defiance was for them faith.

The emotional upheaval was an unraveling. I was swept from one corner of my beliefs to another, never remaining long in one place. I was driven on by an awakening of sexual desire, by self-pity as well as courage, by a sense of reprieve and the impulse to abandon—a spiritual revolution. The carefully maintained barrier of my emotional distance with Camilla and others and the strict dichotomies around which my judgments occurred daily without reflection had shrunk by dawn to irrelevancy.

I knew enough of the lives of Rosa and Martín, remembered mostly from the popular but improbable hagiographies of my childhood, to understand how the relationship revealed in their letters might have come about and to accept the plausibility of everything set out in them. Martín was born in 1579, Rosa seven years later. She lived in a house with ten brothers and sisters on Calle de Santo Domingo, adjacent to the Dominican monastery Martín entered as a lay helper when he was fifteen. Rosa's mother, Maria de Flores, was an irritable, hot-tempered woman. Her father, who participated as a professional soldier in the defeat of the Pizarros at Jaquijahuana, later became superintendent of the silver mines at Quives. Rosa helped support the family by selling flowers she raised in a garden that shared a wall with the monastery gardens Martín de Porres attended.

Rosa was canonized in 1671. Sainthood for Martín did not come until 1962—a delay caused, some say, by the fact that he was dark-skinned. The transcribed testimony of their contemporaries, provided to apostolic tribunals convened at the time of each one's death, is explicit and almost without contradiction concerning the holiness of each person. The extent of their charity toward the destitute, the injured, the abandoned, was then and remains for us now unfathomable. The infusion of physical comfort and spiritual solace each conveyed to ease every kind of human suffering was so inexplicable, so unearthly, it must be regarded as miraculous. A striking sign of their blessedness is that both Rosa and Martín were repeatedly discovered elevated three or four feet off the ground before the Crucifix in a state of spiritual ecstasy or oblivion.

At the time of their ministries, life for many in Lima was an unmitigated horror. The city teemed with gangs of orphans. Epidemic disease was rampant. The many victims of the depraved and bloody administration of the Spanish viceroyalty lived crowded in hovels throughout the city and swarmed the streets for the garbage and waste on which they survived. Reading records of that time, one is soon confirmed in the belief that this was a period of human derangement—the whipping of Church-owned slaves, the public rape of street urchins. It was into this debilitating and sordid atmosphere that Rosa and Martín were born and in which each developed a sense of God.

Of the two, Rosa was the more reclusive. At the age of thirteen she came to believe adamantly that only by devoting herself to prayer, to the most abject supplication before God, might she find salvation. She cut herself off from human society, embarked on a period of harsh fasts, and regularly beat herself with sticks. Her many chroniclers are at pains to describe her self-flagellation as "masochistic and abnormal," but looking at the letters and the entirety of her life, I believe her behavior was instead an act of rage against the darkness manifest in the streets around her and which she also saw in herself. Her biographers refer to these seven years as her "period of aridity." It was near the end of this time that she met Martín.

The Dominican friar was much more outgoing, a humorous, energetic man, the son of an hidalgo named Juan de Porres and of Anna Velasquez, a Panamanian woman variously described as an Indian and as a free black. Martín lived the impoverished life of a religious abject but was so enthusiastic about human life and so ready with self-deprecating jokes that he confounded those who piously recorded his miraculous cures of the terminally ill. Each day he walked out into the streets of Lima to help whomever he met. Like Rosa, who turned her parents' home into a hospice for abused prostitutes, Martín brought the most deracinated and wretched back to the monastery, housing them in his own small cell if necessary. His charity was celebrated throughout Lima; the wealthy sought his counsel and showered him with money.

During the months in which the letters were written, in the fall of 1606, I think, Rosa was twenty. She was just entering a period of serenity in her life, a time of transcendent beatitude such as people often imagine to be the equanimity of angels. It lasted until she died in 1617, at the age of thirty-one. Martín would have been twenty-seven in 1606. Among his official duties at the monastery were his responsibilities in the hospital and in the garden, but he spent much of his time in the streets. In a city blighted by ambitious schemes and cruel enforcements, he was for all the pariahs an elevating hand, a sympathetic ear.

Rosa and Martín, lacking a certain cupidity and the designs of power that would have drawn them more completely into the world, nevertheless willingly engaged in its terrors. Against holiness like theirs one has no recourse, no protection. It was part of the reason I broke down that night.

I slept most of the day after my night of reading and catharsis. The following day Camilla and Manco went to Callao to visit his grandmother, and I had the house to myself. I took out the nine letters my father had given me and read them for the first time in many years. I had then a sudden, intuitive sense of the order of all the letters. Assembled along these lines they revealed a clear evolution of psychological and spiritual ideas.

The letters my father gave me seem all to have been among the earliest written. Their composers describe with wonder and joy each other's smallest physical attributes. They dwell on the blinding ecstasy produced by mere touch—the inside of the wrist, say, lifting the bare flesh of the breast. Rosa writes of the heat and the pressure she experiences straining against him, the sensation of his penetration she feels in her spine, the delirious loss of her mind. Martín writes of the inexplicable tears that wet their faces, the thrill of restraint and hesitation in his tongue drawn across the shuddering currents of her skin. They make love in her garden most often. In their letters they speculate at the way they tear plants from the ground in their ravishment and at her compulsion to ride him like a horse, and they recall how in a kiss Martín had unfurled honey against her teeth and then slowly caressed every part of her mouth he could reach.

In those early letters they seem to affirm not physical passion so much as entry upon a form of reverie both familiar and unknown to them, a capacity for such experience that for them must have been an abiding hunger. In subsequent letters (the majority of these from the library) they explore the meaning of this elevated state, and they consider the unity they have discovered through it—with each other, with jasmine blossoms that fall on them in the garden, and with their spiritual calling, the prayer and ministration that shaped the hours of their daily lives.

It's my feeling that I have read most of the letters they wrote, that there were few earlier or later ones. The letters originate in the realm of physical sensation, move to a more ethereal realm (though still rooted in the physical), and culminate in what appears to be the completion of an understanding of what they were striving for. I would guess that all of the letters were written during a period of only two or three months, and I see the evidence of this intense companionship most clearly in a change in Rosa's life. Certain references in the letters suggest that Martín prevailed upon Rosa to cease beating herself. Rosa had as profound an effect, I think, on Martín's life, though this is harder to discern. If Rosa's "period of aridity" came to an end during these months, this, too, was possibly the time that Martín acquired the gift that permitted him to speak to animals. Before this, his love had embraced even the most wounded human being; following upon his intimacy with Rosa, the tenderness he exhibited was undiscriminating and unbounded. It extended toward all life.

In what I feel was the final letter, Rosa tells Martín that as a sign of their love, of the "elimination of the barriers that exclude God," they should regularly place vases of flowers on the garden wall, where the arrangements would be visible to each of them. Indeed, in statements included in testimony taken down by the apostolic tribunals, I've found references to the fact that until their last day it was the habit of each of these people to place bouquets of flowers on their common wall, the instances of this noted because no matter what the season, vivid displays of lilies and roses appeared.

The letters of Rosa and Martín have compelled my salvation, but they have also created a dilemma for me. My foremost responsibility, I believe, is to protect them from fanatics, from obliteration or derision. (Curious, how late in life has come the realization of what my father meant.) In the days following my discovery of the letters in the library, however, I developed such an affection toward the world, such a sense of tenderness toward anyone caught in the predicament of life, that I came to view publication of the letters as an urgent matter. By means of this one gesture, I thought, so much of the putrefaction and hypocrisy of evil could be wiped away. I now saw the physical attraction between my students, Pedro and Analilia, not as mundane carnality but as unperfected desire, and within that a potential for pervading love, whether or not they decided to marry. With Camilla, whom I had become so remote from, who had become almost an idea to me, I rediscovered simple sensual pleasure. Perhaps most striking for me was the recovery of a sense of the vastness of the world outside my own concerns and aspirations.

What would seem astonishing to a modern reader of these letters, of course, is that two saints embraced the physical hunger that enveloped them instead of running from it. They took it as a sign of God. Then, riding a wave of passion large enough to drown most of us, they transmuted that clutching, compressing, exhausting physical love into a deeper knowledge of God, achieving a peace in their own lives that they gave away in all the dark corners of Lima.

Even as I saw the good that could come from publishing the letters, however, I knew it was being realistic rather than cynical to see that any such publication in Peru would be suppressed, or so thoroughly undermined that the letters would finally be dismissed as forgeries. The Church would call it blasphemy, Hollywood would beat at the door with money and offer solemn promises. The endurance of these letters through fourteen generations would then culminate in an explosion. They would fall back to the earth like so much confetti.

By some means, however, I intend to release these letters. It is amazing that love like this is the experience of saints, but the apparatus of sainthood and Catholicism, it seems to me, is not essential in the story of these people, only knowledge of the spiritual life to be found at the core of their physical experience. Ecstasy seems directionless to me, but like all passion, it might be directed toward the divine.

I am considering several courses of action. If I forward copies of the letters to a friend in China, a scholar of religion at the University of Wuhan, he could arrange for their publication there. They would then emerge as a kind of heresy and so enjoy that protection. I am also considering paying for their publication in Lima under the auspices of a spurious monastery in Catalonia. Eventually they would be discredited by the Church as a work of fiction, but they would suffer less that way than if the authorities were forced to treat them as a reality.

The letters, of course, have given me my first understanding of the humanity of saints. I've written out passages from them on small slips of paper which I meditate upon during Mass. For example, in one letter Martín describes how he wishes to place his lips in a depression above Rosa's clavicle and draw from it the poisonous residue left by her father's beatings, which she had endured as a child. In another letter Rosa speaks of the power of memory to kindle desire when presented with a certain scene—the undulating flight of swallows reminds her of the swoon of physical ecstasy, the overlapping songs of finches in the garden at dawn restore the sensation of his first touch.

For now, I will keep the letters I took from the library. I don't know how to resolve the theft, but it can wait until I see a way through this larger responsibility. I've never discussed the letters with Camilla. I have not discussed them with my eldest son, Artaud, though I am actually inclined to pass them on to our middle child, Elouisa. She has a quick, irreverent mind, but she is the most principled person in the family and contains, I suspect, the deepest waters. I consider that it has fallen to me only to have made this additional discovery in the university library, to complete the collection of letters. Now that their meaning is so clear, it may be for Elouisa to determine our next step.

When Camilla and I were courting, I took images from the letters to astonish and impress her. I now believe this the only sin, the one failure of integrity that I persisted in with these letters. It filled me with such shame that I later confessed the sin many times, to be forgiven again and again.

One evening I will ask Camilla to go for a walk with me. I hope to direct us to some place along the Río Rímac, a spot where the other two might once have stood.

Mornings in Quarain

The two gentlemen behind me are speaking fervently of a mining venture, which holds for each of them a promise of long-sought wealth; but my attention is drawn, again, to the one hundred macaws in the garden. (Last night when I arrived at the hotel, I didn't notice that change, not in the silence and darkness beyond the deserted lobby. When I came into the breakfast room this morning, the animated stretching of wings and bold display of color on the other side of the glass wall were unexpected, intriguing.) The two men are in such high spirits about the prospects of their enterprise that I turn to eavesdrop. Asterquerite is what they're talking about, a rare compound found occasionally with other siliceous minerals on the peninsula. (I originally read about it in something my mother wrote. It has no industrial application, as I recall, so is of no commercial value.)

The macaws are a long way from home—the scarlets, perhaps from Venezuela, with their blue, green, and yellow wings and red tails, and the deep iron-blue hyacinths from the interior of Brazil. Their crisp, vivid dress seems an extension of the perfectly appointed table before me, starched linen, Royal Doulton china. A ripe casaba melon I've just begun is succulent as honeycomb. The coffee is dark and robust.

The birds, with their shank hook bills and long, tapering tails, appear regal in the limbs of young eucalyptus (the hyacinths roosting higher up), but they twitch and glare, as if puzzled by the precipitous disappearance of a familiar horizon.

It is becoming clearer from my companions' ardent conversation that astequerite has a new-wrought, esoteric application at a mill in France. They concur that their profits could be considerable if they can perfect a route unencumbered by delay between the Arabian peninsula and buyers in France. The process will require many permits, perhaps a good deal of money.

The sun has risen over the hotel's Spanish tile roof. In this more incisive light, the large birds are dazzling, garnets and lapis lazuli. They shift about crankishly, as if the thought of flight has now occurred to them.

I am savoring melted butter sunk in the lightly toasted texture of an English muffin when my two friends suddenly begin to wrestle with large paper maps, refolding them into manageable sizes, pursuing their conversation from one region to another. (The breakfast room is large but only one other table is occupied, two Arab men across the way, waiting for someone, I think.)

The waitress could hardly be more attentive, more polite. She asks, would I enjoy another piece of melon. Just a small slice? she smiles. I have eaten the first with such appreciation, I tell her, that to order another would seem crass. I ask, does she know anything about the macaws? No, she apologizes, she knows nothing.

One of the Arabs is scarfed in thick, languid smoke from his cigarette. He wears dark glasses, a short, black leather jacket, and for long moments at a time he stares either at his ashtray or the ceiling. The man across from him, dressed in a white jubbah, the white kaffiyeh on his head held in place with a maroon agal, has been speaking an unbroken aqueous stream of Arabic into a portable telephone, a muted harangue, which every so often breaks through the emphatic conversation of the men behind me.

"Monsieur? You have a question about the parrots?"

A young man in a dark suit and green tie steps aside with self-conscious formality to permit the waitress to place a bowl of Swiss muesli in front of me with a small pitcher of milk.

"Yes, you know about them?"

"A little, sir."

"I was curious: it's only hyacinths and scarlets?"

"Correct, just the two. Exactly one hundred of them, twenty-five each, male and female."

"I see; it's a stunning sight. I hope you won't find this indecent, but I'm also curious, with all the freedom they have to fly, how—"

"Overhead, sir, we have—"

"Yes, yes, I see the net, I know they can't get out, but what

I'm wondering is, how do you manage with the swimming pool? And the lounge chairs? I mean, it's very clean."

"Oh, yes. Everything here is quite spotless. You don't have to be concerned at all. You will want a swim this morning?"

"No, what I mean is, the birds, they don't . . . you know. . . ."

"Oh! Oh, no sir, they don't. That has been taken care of. They go to just one place for that."

"How do you get them to do it?"

"Lights, sir. Do you see the blue light there, at the corner of the roof? And that one over there? Every twenty minutes those lights blink, and the birds that have a necessity fly to their place."

"Which place is that?"

"Just behind there, sir." He steps around me to point discreetly but sharply at a spot above a bamboo thicket. "No one can see."

"Yes. I understand now. But birds this large, they also eat a lot of fruit. They carry it around. What do you do about all the rinds and pits?"

"Rinds and pits?"

"Do you have another place where they eat?"

"Oh, yes! I'm sorry! In those trees, you see that platform with the slanting sticks? They feed inside there—but to get out, they can't take anything with them. It's an ingenious quality built into the design. You will find the rinds and pits in there."

"This has been very helpful. Thank you."

"Not at all, monsieur."

My mother once wrote a story for *The New Yorker* about a Saudi sheik who collected psittacine birds. He responded to her questions, she told me, in enraptured language, dwelling on the subtlety and brilliance of their coloring, lingering over the attractiveness of their movements. The way she conveyed his passion in the article made his interest seem erotic. He collected the rare, the colorful: rainbow lorikeets and turquoise parrots from Australia; Rueppell's parrot from Namibia; plum-headed parakeets from India. He sent a private jet to retrieve the rarest ones, she wrote, a bronze phase St. Vincent parrot, once, from that Caribbean island. It was during this conversation with her, in fact, after the article appeared, that I first raised the issue of the style of her writing and the Muslim world. Her tone and her approach with the birds, I offered, might not sit well with some people.

She smiled, tolerant, a sardonic edge to the smile, and said, "They'll never study what a woman has to say about birds and sand dunes, not in some foreign magazine."

But, of course, they did.

My two friends with the maps, now on their fifth or sixth cup of coffee, seem close to agreement on a day plan, what each man's responsibilities will be. The men at the other table persevere without change, one beclouded in dense smoke, the other speaking vehemently into his cellular phone and making abrupt, impatient gestures with his hands.

Yesterday, from Frankfurt, I called Faisal Abu-Said in Riyadh, confirming our appointment; now, pressing milk from the last spoonful of coarse muesli against the roof of my mouth, I feel a familiar doubt: I'm no more certain he'll arrive this time than I was the others.

My neighbors are shaking hands, briskly reassuring each other, agreeing to meet in the lobby at six. (I look up at the blue light on the roof. It is flashing, about thirty macaws have taken wing. They flock, screeching, to an area behind a bamboo thicket.) At the second table the man on the phone has rung off. He sits frowning, looking distant, opposite his very grave and silent companion.

Sunlight cutting through the glass, the air like wool in the room, would have made me drowsy of an afternoon. This early in the morning I find the closeness, the light, auspicious. I ask the waitress for a large glass of fresh orange juice, and could she serve it outside?

My mother first came to Arabia in the 1950s. She had been a friend of Bowles in New York. She visited him in Tangier, but was soon drawn away to the emirates of what was then Trucial Oman and to Saudi Arabia. She traveled to spectacular, remote places to write—the great salt lagoon at Umm as Samīm, south of Ibri, and up to the ruins at Petra. She was didactically romantic about Baghdad, that it had once flourished as a city of poets and scholars under Harun al-Rashid and was unrivaled as a settlement in the Muslim world in the ninth century, and she would say that she could never visit Baghdad because it would dismantle that illusion of civilization. She wrote a well-received biography of William Palgrave, a Jesuit and the first outsider to cross the Arabian peninsula. She wrote to Camus about his emotions over Algeria and kept up a correspondence with the Englishman Thesiger, the last explorer of Rub' al-Khali, the Empty Quarter. She disdained, out of jealousy, the popular reports and impressions of Lady Anne Blunt, the first European woman to travel in the interior of Arabia, sometimes in native male disguise.

Mother wore long pants and traveled as a Christian. She had a scholar's inclination toward detail and great passion for her subjects, also a physical longing for the desert I admired, though it never developed for me, nor my father. I read most of what she wrote with deference and fascination. When she was killed, in Basra in 1984, one of the first thoughts I had was for the safety of her manuscripts and diaries at her home in Riyadh. But her killers had gotten to them. She had moved overseas when my father died. Eventually she consolidated all of her work in the home in Riyadh. She lived an urgent, forceful life with that city as her base. It wasn't until I visited her there that I could understand how she managed to gain trust, even affection, as an interloper. Muslim people, everywhere I traveled, appreciated her ingenuous interest—except, of course, the reactionary fanatics who rigged the gas explosion in her kitchenette.

Abu-Said ran to her house that same day, the moment he heard, but he arrived to find it ransacked. Her manuscripts, her books, all her notes—all the paper was gone. When I reflected later on what happened, I grew angry with my mother. I had reminded her pointedly, several times, of the fate of such well-meaning people as Ulrich Seetzen, an intrepid student of Arab culture murdered at Ta'izz. His journals were publicly shredded and burned on the spot.

Two years after she was killed, I got a letter from Abu-Said saying Mother's papers may not have been destroyed. He had been contacted. It may take a lot of money, he told me, but it was just possible to get them back. I told him he must try. I had read a little in her journals, pages of curious speculation and glee, of marvelous coincidence, much less guarded than her essays. To me, the loss of her musings was a loss almost as great as her death. I raised some money from her colleagues and an interested university, and over the next six years Abu-Said negotiated. I kept a growing sense of frustration to myself. In 1988 I flew to Quarain for my first meeting with Abu-Said. I waited three days at the hotel before flying back to the States, where I found a letter saying it was an inauspicious time for us to get together, that he was sorry but he could not finally do so.

The letter had been delayed.

The next time, 1991, I waited for two days, again at the hotel. The garden where the macaws are now was then dense with hibiscus, jasmine, and frangipani. I was sitting in that nearly overpowering perfume finishing breakfast when Abu-Said approached and sat down. He was cordial and apologetic—and empty-handed. He reiterated what sort of people we were dealing with and promised not to give up. I wondered whether he and Mother had been lovers, if this was an added complication, and was then abashed at the narrowness of my imagination.

The man with the cellular phone has placed another call. He now seems calmer. His companion crushes out perhaps his tenth cigarette as I rise to find a seat in the garden. At that moment a nagging question is put away: the breakfast room is almost empty because it is Ramadan, the month of fasting.

Outside, the screeching and harsh cries of the disturbed

macaws are no longer muffled by the double-glass wall. A difficult decision to have to make, I speculate, opting for the brilliance of these birds' markings and their impressive size in spite of the scabrous grate of their calls. The soft warble and chatter of other types of smaller but still brightly colored parrots might have been more agreeable around a hotel pool, but someone has decided the overall image would be less striking.

The cold orange juice, thick with pulp, perpetuates an exotic sense of prosperity: fresh, chilled food eaten early in the day at the edge of Rub' al-Khali. But the hotel is a peculiar oasis. Like everyone else at this Tiergarten, I expect an array of imported fruit each morning, the extravagance with water, with linen, the exaggerated courtesy.

I am taking a second sip from the sweating glass when I see Abu-Said emerge on a walkway from behind a screen of flowering oleander. He is carrying a leather case—much too small—but he is smiling.

After we shake hands lightly, he places the wallet on the table between us and asks if I have slept well. We exchange such perfunctory remarks until this object entirely fills our silences. The wallet contains a letter, he says. He tells me to have written it was dangerous, and very brave. It is addressed to me, to read, not to keep.

Abu-Said waves away the approaching waitress as I undo the leather ties and remove a sheet of heavy, cream-colored paper, folded once and written on one side.

"To the Son of Frances Amelia Desuedeson," it begins.

We cannot console you or make explanations for what has happened but some among us also admired your mother for her humility and for her enthusiasm for Islam and our land. What she wrote was in certain places wrong and offensive to us, but the ways of Allah are complicated beyond our understanding. Some of what she wrote was indeed beautiful to our ears. We do not all of us agree but are now willing to make a gift of these papers to you. We ask you to go back to your home, not to come again to Quarain, and never to publish these papers. What inspires us we cannot explain to you, and you should not try to explain us to anyone. We do not live in the time you are living in.

The letter was unsigned. I read it again. I was afraid if I looked at Abu-Said, I would sense the years that had passed. I suddenly felt the selfishness of my errand, the inadequacy of my mission.

Abu-Said leaned over and said, "If you are finished, put the letter back in the case. When I go I will leave a room key on the table. In that room, tomorrow morning at ten o'clock, you will find two suitcases with your mother's papers. At exactly two p.m. you are to take them to the Lufthansa cargo office at the airport. A man there will assist you in making arrangements to get the bags to Frankfurt. After that, you are on your own."

At that moment it seemed I could not draw in enough of something, of the pungent odor of flower blossoms in the quivering air, the intense chroma of the birds' hues, the density of the orange juice. I raised my hand to stay Abu-Said, who had started to rise. I wanted an explanation. I put the letter in the case and knotted the leather ties.

"It is not good for me to visit much longer," Abu-Said cautioned.

"I understand," I said. "I regret that I can't make a copy of the letter, but I won't ask you for that. I regret, too, that we cannot enjoy some of the day together before you go. I have no way to thank you for what you've done. You never gave up."

"Nor did you," he said. He waited.

"Did you love her very much?" I finally asked.

"I did, with my whole heart."

"May Allah bless you every day."

"And may you arrive home safely, if it be Allah's will."

We touched hands. He nodded once and walked quickly away. Somewhere, I felt, he had paid a price.

I finished my juice, signed the check, and took the key. I would spend the rest of the morning walking in the city before the heat became intolerable, looking in the shops. Tomorrow, before I went to the room, I would have breakfast at the same table. I would order the same things and watch the macaws stretching their bright wings in the pale dawn air.

The Construction
of the Rachel

What she said to me was "I've met someone." What I heard was "I'm leaving." She was correct, of course, from her side, but that's what it came down to for me and soon I, too, was gone. I don't know whether it was indecision or cowardice that, instead of quitting, led me to take a leave of absence from the firm in which I was a full partner; but I said so long there, closed the house and drove south out of Boise into Nevada, where I thought there would be enough space to work through the first layers of the injury. For long stretches in Nevada there are no towns, and I carried no cell phone or pager. I drove some roads where there was no fence to either side, no power line crossing the horizon.

The dog after me was grief, not bitterness. It had not worked; now that she had taken the first step, I would have to find my own path. I began to think through things I had been walking away from for years. One hour I felt like an utter fool, the next like a man given a legal reprieve. As I stared through the windshield or into the cottage-cheese ceilings of cheap motels or into cafe-counter mirrors, I saw with some clarity what had happened. My ruminations were not about blame or responsibility. Outside of the loneliness, the violent shivers of anger and general fury at the world, I traveled in peace. I could not bear to read anything and did not want conversation, only to get on with what was coming. If desperation was in me, it was to keep reminding myself on those rueful and sleepless nights of what was possible. And if I returned regularly to any single image, it was to that long arc of time and event from childhood to the present. What was in that I could depend on?

I was at this a few months, eating breakfast at five in some fluorescent-lit cafe with cattle ranchers and no women except those serving; smoking an occasional cigar on the lawn of some off-the-highway motel, gazing at the last direct rays of the sun sparkling high in a rampart of Lombardy poplars and hearing children shouting their glee and irritation from the motel pool. The desire to read returned as abruptly as it had left. One day I picked up a copy of John McPhee's *Basin and Range*. I read it in the evenings, gaining his sense of deep time to understand the dynamism of a landscape that seems the quintessence of stillness. As I drove, I began to appreciate the geology I was traversing, the clines and faults, and to see its basins and ranges like the crests and troughs of a stalled ocean.

One evening I looked up from my reading by a motel pool and saw in the middle ground of my imagination a monk in white robes. He was bending over to comfort a child in a cloister.

The Benedictine monastery of San José de Galisteo stands on a low knoll in the Santa Lucia Range of the central California Coast. I had known of it since my boyhood in Santa Barbara, and in recent years had visited there. I found the monks worldly, funny, compassionate, and cerebral. Nominally Catholic, they were open to any genuine search for the divine. One afternoon, walking in the garden with the prior, Brother Jorge, and talking about the rationale behind Buchenwald and Treblinka, he offered one of his typically succinct summaries. "Liturgy without justice is sentimentality. And justice without liturgy is barbarism."

My visits with the monks had been as comforting as my recent weeks in the Triassic folds of Nevada. Why I'd not gone there first I didn't know. I was there a week or two before I saw the outline of something else in the long run of beach below the monastery. That margin represented a boundary for me, one I could not have found without swimming across Nevada.

I could easily have paid the small fee the monks suggested to cover my meals and laundry and been done with it; but I needed another sort of exchange, and I wanted to be physically engaged in the world again. I arranged with Brother Thomas to work under his direction in the monastery's gardens. They raised vegetables and fruits for their own table and sold what remained in a public market in Paso Robles on the weekend.

As on earlier visits, I asked to live under a rule of silence, speaking and being spoken to only on Sundays. Brother Thomas wrote out my chores and left his list each day on a small table in the courtyard garden where I usually ate alone. I attended canonical hours with the monks, starting with matins at four a.m. and continuing through compline at eight-thirty, giving my day that spine. Observing the three meal-times, attending the seven hours, and receiving the Eucharist at noon was the daily order I needed. Around it I weeded, trimmed, picked, and gathered. I read and slept deeply.

I held to this rhythm for weeks, speaking with the brothers on Sundays or going for a long hike, and then reentering my silence on Sunday evening. Outside of birdsong, wind in the bare branches, and the click and snip of my tools, all I heard was the opening and closing of doors, the sound of footsteps on wood floors, and the tick of utensils in the dining room. On Sunday we talked about baseball, about the ruins at Petra, and of the defiant natures of Isadora Duncan, Artaud, and O'Keeffe.

This tranquil, innocent mantra ended one day with a frightful disturbance. Every evening the monks lock the outer doors of the quadrangle that forms the monastery, even though the monastery's remoteness and its very nature make it unlikely that thieves would enter. One night after compline, while I was reading in the library, Brother Elliott handed me a note saying, "If you go outside, please be sure to lock the door when you return." His note irritated me. Why did I need to be reminded?

I did go outside that night, exiting through the library door in the north wall of the monastery and crossing a wide driveway to a low stone wall that marked the edge of a bluff above the ocean. The night was clear. I could see the arc of the Milky Way and thought I could discern the evidence of all that starlight on the enormous heave of the ocean. A few long minutes, though, and I was ready for bed. As I turned back toward the library door, which I had pulled to behind me, I saw a creature about the size of a spaniel run from the edge of the building. It angled away from me across the drive, moving swiftly to the bluff wall. My jaw quivered involuntarily as I studied the space in the dark where it crossed. As it rose to the low wall, the hair on my arms and head stiffened. It was the movement of an animal without legs. It slipped away down the wall around some overhanging bushes, and then slid down and seemed to lope off into open country behind the monastery, into the steep canyons of the Santa Lucia.

This all happened in a few seconds. I moved quickly to the door, my head trembling in denial. Bolting through the opening, I nearly tore the library door from its hinges trying to lock it behind me. All the way to my room I felt a weight like a wet hawser of darkness lying along my spine, and trailing my body like a tail.

In the days following, I felt the contrary presence of the world leaning forcefully against the idyllic existence I had contrived. I put Brother Elliott's note in my journal.

I started having trouble sleeping around this time, and I grew afraid that I would not be able to sleep again, for I now more easily fell prey to that sort of self-doubt that dismantles the first stages of every attempt to recover one's balance in the wake of a great loss. I did not, of course, find rapport with every one of the monks. A few seemed unaware from the beginning—men ignoring the world; others seemed to have penetrated the world and to have arrived somewhere from which they could now look back and be a kind of beacon for the rest of us. What I admired in each one, though, was that in their Rule of St. Benedict they had found a kind of psychological order they had the wisdom not to disturb. They had been leaning into it for centuries. It wasn't religion, and it was their first great gift to me.

I lay awake a few hours before matins one night, turning every couple of minutes trying to find the entry port to sleep, to squeeze through into oblivion, and imagined a ship I had built as a boy, a model of the windjammer *Cutty Sark* sailing through the ceiling. I'd taken pride in building that ship because I had successfully strung every line of the standing and running rigging (and I had finished it without sails to trumpet the feat); but all I saw that night was its hull cutting the water. I saw it from below as a diver would, the sleek parabolas, hyperbolas, and ellipses of the hull lines ripping through the ocean, the cleave of the entry and the afterboil of its wake as the wind above bent twenty-some sails, from the main courses to the moonrakers, and the refined invention bore on, its caulked and nailed materials shuddering just this side of flying apart, but so well conceived and built that it ran like a dolphin.

In the moment it surged over my head I fell into sleep.

The silence of the monastery and the privacy it afforded made me wonder after a while what the other monks actually did during the day. I hardly saw them, except for Brother Thomas. When I asked, Brother Jorge said Brother Aloysius built furniture in a basement workshop; Brother Raymond repaired bound books in another place; Brother Timothy and Brother Fadius volunteered as nurses in hospitals in Atascadero and Morro Bay; and Brother Emmett wrote detective novels. He said that Brother Maria was basically a surfer, but that he also helped Brother Aloysius, and that the other brothers were mostly occupied with tasks around the monastery and with helping AIDS patients and indigents. Brother Jorge himself was writing a ninth volume in his *History of Mexico*.

I told Brother Jorge, partly to define a task of my own, that I had decided to build a large model, a ship. I asked if he had some space in which I could work. He described a small room off the kitchen he said I could have, if I could find somewhere to store the flour and other staples. He thought of this room, he said, because it had a window with a view to the sea.

The monastery building was originally constructed as a palacial home, with a ballroom, art and sculpture galleries, and a library. A financier from Kansas City had it built in 1957, but when his wife died he found he didn't want to live in it alone and I believe he all but gave it to Brother Jorge. He wasn't a Catholic, but he apparently had great respect for Brother Jorge's intellect and spirituality. Whatever thoughts he had had of spending years in retirement in the place with his beloved wife, he successfully transmuted them into years lived here by Brother Jorge and the other monks.

When, in that same conversation about the room, I told Brother Jorge about the creature I'd seen, he smiled and gave me a look of acknowledgment and assurance, his raised eyebrows saying I had at that moment stepped briefly into waters in which he rowed every day. (What made me trust Brother Jorge was that at odd hours I would find him smoking a cigarette in the gardens while he pulled weeds with his free hand.)

I had been thinking about ships ever since I'd dreamed about the *Cutty Sark*'s hull cutting through the ceiling. I wanted to build a *ship*, not a bark or a schooner, but a square-rigged, three-masted ship, a model of Cook's *Resolution* or a working ship like the whaler *Charles W. Morgan*, or one of the storied clippers, like the *Flying Cloud*. I wanted to build an object that would make more real the longing to get somewhere, to do something.

I finally settled on a model of the *Rachel*, a ship built in Mystic, Connecticut, in 1851. She had worked as a grainer, mostly, carrying hard wheat from California to Hong Kong and Djakarta and then chinaware and tea and teak lumber on the back haul. I got a set of plans through the mail and in Morro Bay bought the few tools I would need. I wrote out an order for spars, decking, strakes, rigging, and other parts, but then quickly shortened it. I had another idea, and sent out only for chain and sails.

The *Rachel* carried twenty-one sails: three jib sails forward and a spanker rigged fore and aft on the mizzen mast at the rear of the ship; five square sails each on the fore and main masts and another four on the mizzen. Between the fore and main masts she was rigged with two staysails, and between the main and mizzen masts was a third staysail, all three rigged fore and aft, at ninety degrees to the square sails.

As a boy I had had trouble with sails. Each one is slightly different, and I could never cut them exactly right. I planned to mount these furled, but I wanted them absolutely right before I lashed them up to their yards.

I kept at my work in the garden with Brother Thomas, but made additional time now in my daily routine to get down to the beach for a walk. One day in the wrack line I found a ball cap, which I took to wearing against the sun. Another time I found a door with an ornate set of latch plates, a confirmation of the other part of my plan. With bits of plastic thrown up on the beach and scraps of clothing, and with the great supply of driftwood and odd bits of metal attached to this debris, I thought I could fashion everything else I needed for the *Rachel*, from deck planking to its binnacle and water buckets. What I could not find on the beach I might locate around the monastery—broken clocks and radios, say, from which I could take the materials for capstans and rudder hinges.

It would take longer than buying everything ready-made, but it was the better route.

Embarking on this task altered the shape of my day for the third time since I'd left Boise. Deep within the pattern of canonical hours and the times set for meals, I built a rhythm of work that included gardening, walking the wrack line on the beach, and working on the ship. Though repetitive and predictable, the rhythm was engaging, like riding a gaited horse through ever-changing country.

I set up in the room Brother Jorge assigned me. The day the plans arrived, I laid them out on the worktable like oracular documents. I lifted measurements for the hull design from the plans with a pair of dividers and tried them out on various pieces of wood I had gathered. I saw quickly that I had enough hawthorn branches to fashion the ship's frames. I had a limb of applewood from the beach from which I could saw the thirty-one-inch keel and the stem and stern posts. I read the ship plans like a property list for a play. I had scraps of isinglass to use for the skylight above the captain's quarters. I had a broken car antenna to slice for spar rings.

I'd not built a model ship in twenty-five years, but the skills were still in my hands, and more importantly, I still had a sense of how to manage the sequence of steps, so I wouldn't, say, install the main mast with its shrouds and stays and, in so doing, block access to additional work required on that part of the deck. I had been able to obtain a set of used surgical tools—hemostats, scalpels, needle probes—through Brother Fadius, which simplified many tasks requiring precision and dexterity. I was also able to assemble a set of used dental tools to the same end, a related discovery made in my youth.

I wanted the ship to come quickly, but of course it didn't. Many hours into the work, I would wonder what had happened to my once certain sense of its impending completion. Making the incredible array of ropes and cordage I needed—halliards, sheets, clew garnets, vangs, lifts, braces, guys, brails, tacks—each one different from the others, took weeks instead of days to get right. And, of course, things went together wrong, and work had to be taken apart, and things broke; and then one day when I was so angry I snapped an unpainted pencil in my fist, I saw in the fragments the six-sided spool piece I needed for a winch on the forward deck. I readjusted my chair. And I began again.

The day I glued in the last hull plank, which for the first time revealed the exquisite distillation of curves that allowed the ship to run so smoothly through the water, Brother Jorge was standing in my door. (Though it was a Sunday, the monks never presumed you wished to be interrupted, let alone spoken to, just because it was Sunday. During the week they never so much as made eye contact with me unless we were involved in coordinating a task together.) But there he was, with his heavy-rimmed glasses and his finger in a book folded to his chest.

"Is it ready?" he asked.

"Well, just now, as you come by, the hull is finished. I have the masts, the rigging, the decking and deck equipment and furniture, all that to go."

"May I look?"

"Oh my, yes, of course."

I pushed back from the table and he approached as if he were about to inspect a being. He laid his book aside on the table and bent in close. I watched his eye as it took in the flow of planks, from the garboard strake at the keel all the way to the sheer strake at the deck, and the longitudinal lines fore and aft, from the bow through the beam to the stern. His look was not of approval but one of confoundment and wonder.

"Who thought of this?"

"Of ships?"

"No, of this design, this line?"

"Do you want a complicated answer?"

"Yes."

"When the East India Company, in England, lost its charter, and ships began competing to get from one port to another, speed became of the essence. Naval architects tried to find new solutions to drag and resistance, and the first great solution was a clipper ship called the *Ann McKim*, built in Baltimore in eighteen thirty-two. By the time the *Cutty Sark* was built in eighteen sixty-nine, they were approaching speeds of close to eighteen knots, nearly twice as fast as the old ships."

"Capitalism?"

"Mmm. The desire for profit, competition in a free market. It produced the need for the clippers, but the ships were things of beauty without that. When steam came along, ships got much uglier. The graceful lines here in the hull became bloated and square so the ships could carry more cargo."

"Are you saying that the beauty of the ship, then, was a kind of accident, that it didn't need to be beautiful?"

"Yes."

"And so, when its days had passed, ships like this, they had nothing to do? They became orphans, relics?"

"Yes."

"Not capitalism, then. I think it must have been the desire for beauty that made the ship, along with the restlessness of the soul, a belief in the solution we say is a journey."

One evening during vespers I realized I had reentered a time of my childhood. I was happy because my energy was almost entirely focused on the ship while the rest of my life was following on like a dog, obedient but unthinking. I put the model aside for a while and concentrated on other parts of what I had now come to think of as my "prayer"—my reading, my Sunday afternoon sessions talking about the history of Mexico with Brother Jorge, my Wednesday mornings with Brother Aloysius in his furniture workshop, my dishwashing and floor-mopping chores.

One day I found a note from Brother Jorge under my door. He'd come upon a reference to sails in the writing of Bartolomé de las Casas, *"las gallardas camisas de los arboles,"* which he translated for me as "the proud shirts of the trees."

I stayed away from the room where I was building the *Rachel* and instead concentrated during those weeks on what was washing up on the beach. I waded in the water, and from time to time swam in the surf, and I walked the mile of sand that stretched before the monastery. I rarely met anyone. One day I found a dollhouse from which I removed a door for a companionway hood. Another day I came upon a dresser drawer, the bottom of which was of a perfect thickness to saw shells for snatch blocks, fiddle blocks, cat blocks, viol blocks, and other exotic parts of the running rigging.

With these and other scraps of raw material to hand, I went back to fashioning ship parts, using jeweler's tools and kerf and bead saws and my medical and dental tools. Making the parts a single one at a time, tapping and tapping a snippet of brass with a tiny hammer on a block of steel, and then drilling it with a needle-thin bit to make a hinge plate, I came back in control of my enormous task.

In the closing weeks of autumn I finished the ship. From jib boom tip to transom it measured thirty-nine inches, and from keel to main masthead twenty-three inches. It rested in cradles screwed to a board of Honduras mahogany, the one piece of wood I took to Brother Aloysius's shop to mill and cut square at his table saw.

In the six months I had been at San José de Galisteo, I had spoken with no one but the monks. Whatever it was I had accomplished at the monastery, I was now ready to return home. I felt cleaned out, not so much healed, I suppose, as capable of managing. I had had no thoughts about whether I would now quit work permanently; but there was a lot of mail waiting, I knew, and no doubt other sorts of messages, and I wanted to attend to it.

I didn't know what to do with the *Rachel*. It was the most beautiful ship I had ever built (which is not saying much, since I was so impatient as a boy with the earlier ships) and I wanted to give it some kind of life. I considered carrying it home, but, more, I needed to release it. As I prepared to leave I thought of a plan, to which Brother Jorge gave his blessing. I would carry it down to the ocean and launch it. Most of it, of course, had come off the beach, from the ocean itself. I would launch it with sails furled, on a morning with a strong offshore breeze. The breeze would carry it out to sea, and then its fate would be its own.

Brother Jorge asked me, as I was preparing to go, if I would set the ship up in one of the wide halls that had once been a gallery, so the other monks could appreciate it outside the confines of the small room where it had come to life. I was glad to. The others smiled and nodded enthusiastically as they inspected it. They wanted me to understand that they thought I'd done a very good job.

The day I chose to launch it, after matins and lauds but before breakfast, I carried the ship down the hill to the shore, with the monks following. I waded into the Pacific with the *Rachel* braced in my arms and stood a while. I teared up at the thought of all the loss in human life, the great and stupid mistakes. I had taken care to ballast the ship and when I set it in the calm water it floated right and square. It rode the water so perfectly that for a moment I felt I was huge and the ship real. I held on to it with one finger hooked over the bulwarks and then let it go. It leaned off under the wind and came around with its stern into the breeze. I glanced back for Brother Jorge, to catch his eye, and saw him standing on the beach with what I knew to be his manuscript of the ninth volume of his *History of Mexico* under his arm. He nodded at me in a way that suggested he was trying to offer reassurance. Behind him the other monks were standing with duffel bags and cloth shopping bags from which loaves of bread and vegetable tops protruded. Brother Damien had arrived in the monastery's blue Ford pickup with a trailer, both piled high with boxes and bundles. They were waving to me, the gesture that says "It's okay, things are fine now," and pointing out to sea.

When I turned back to look for the *Rachel* it was not there but instead, standing offshore, a ship three hundred feet long, its high masts gyrating gently under the morning sky.

I backed away in the water and then plunged ashore to where Brother Jorge stood.

"Again and again," Brother Jorge said to me, "we sailed for Brazil, for the Isles of the Blessed. We sailed until it was no longer possible to sail, because they said the world was known in every corner and men no longer knew how to sail anyway, did not know the names of the sails, the belaying order of the lines. We sailed until men went to sleep at night and let the engines do the work."

As I listened to him I watched Brother Maria, who had stripped to the baggies he always wore under his robes, swimming for the *Rachel*.

"Now we will sail again, Eduardo." He put his manuscript down on top of his leather valise. "Let us help Brother Damien unload the truck."

As we hauled baggage and provisions to the waterline, I watched Brother Maria clamber aboard the ship, swing a boat out on the stern davits, and lower away.

"Do we have enough food here, Father?" asked Brother Theodore.

"Loaves and fishes, my son, loaves and fishes," answered Brother Jorge, smiling at me, hardly looking up from his tasks.

I looked out at the *Rachel*. The water where it rested carried no history to contradict its immediacy or to diminish its right fit on the opaque swells.

In three trips we had every person and every thing aboard. I sent Brother Maria forward with instructions about how to unfurl the sails. He took some of the monks aloft with him on the main mast and began to work. It did not occur to me how we would manage with only the small group of us. As the others began to haul on the sheets and clew lines, I marveled at the abilities of men I had before resigned in my imagination to the world of the monastery. They were adaptable and willing, and lived lives of belief.

I saw Brother Jorge go up to the bows. As the *Rachel* began to respond to the wind, I turned the wheel in my hand to set the angle of the rudder. When I felt the first shallow plunge and race of the hull, I was glad in building the ship I had cut no corner. Not one.

Light Action in the Caribbean

Libby Dalaria had her bags squared up in the hallway next to the door in her apartment by five-forty-five. For the first time since she'd been to Cancún with Brad she was thinking she had everything right, even the underwear. Her only misgivings were about how her dive gear fit, but David had checked out every piece and he'd told her not to worry. Still, she was feeling he really didn't get how everything was supposed to look together, and he'd become really irritated when she said she wanted to get the chartreuse fins, because they had to be special-ordered.

What was important, he had told her, was to have your own things. No rental gear. No wearing other people's stuff. He'd emphasized that and so she'd done it.

So now, she thought, she just had to wait until he showed

up with the cab. She checked the cat food dispenser again and looked over her VCR recording menu. So many shows in a week, she thought, how was she going to watch it all when she got home? She canceled the Julia Roberts special.

David had the passports, he had the tickets, he had the foreign cash. What a relief, she thought. He was so good at this, she could concentrate on things that were going to be important to her. None of them really mattered, she reminded herself, but why not do them right? The book, *Losing Girlfriends*, which Helena had told her was terrific. Her new nighttime skin lotion, Benediction. And she'd replaced all her other lotions with the ozone-calibrated ones. And then vitamins, ginseng, all that. Condoms, in case David forgot. New Wet Maniacs CD. The remastered Bob Marley, to listen to on the plane on the way down, to get into it.

"What a dork," she said out loud, remembering Brad, scanning the street for David and the cab. With him, she thought, she'd have had to do all this for herself, plus figure out the visas, get the tickets, find out what shots Brad needed.

"What a waste," she blurted, staring at small brown stains on her kitchen curtains. Two years with that toad.

David pulled up in the cab. She glanced at her watch. Six a.m. exactly. "I like it," she said.

Driving from Arvada all the way out to the new Denver air-port, thought Libby, was like driving to another country before you could take off. Miles and miles of these nothing fields, no houses, no mountains, no development, no roads, no trees.

"So, where's the airport?" she prompted the driver. "In Kansas?"

"Yeah, right," the cabbie joked back. David gave her a look like she was a jerk. Not cool, she instructed herself.

They were flying United to Miami, then Air Carib to St. Matthew, then Bahía Blanco to San Carlos. It bothered her that most of the way to Miami David gazed into his laptop, but he said there was no way he could arrange the days off without working a little while they were away.

"You are in *command* of your universe," he intoned, closing the laptop firmly and tapping it like a revelatory object. He gave her a look he meant to seem smart and conspiratorial, but which she took to mean he was scheming. At the gate he'd casually thumbed fifty $100 bills in a bank envelope at her.

When they landed, David made cell phone calls from the United gate all the way to the Air Carib gate. She hated being ignored. He said he was just touching base with everyone.

"If you want to be the guy which they cannot do without," he instructed her, "you gotta be sure they really get that. Before they know to ask the question, you answer it. After a while they think of you as indispensable. That's how it works, especially with the programming I'm putting in with these guys. I want them to get a big dose of me before I sign off, and then have them sweat a little next week—"

"Well, that's good."

"So, you know, I screwed a few things up—which they'll run into next week." He gave her a big grin, a smirk he'd seen somewhere, and put his hand up in the air, asking her for a high five.

When they cleared customs in St. Matthew and were waiting at the Bahía Blanco gate, she got out a copy of *Allure*. She'd been reading "Boff Your Breasts for the Boardroom?" for only a few minutes when he said, "So, what, I'm a freaking bore?"

She closed the magazine and slid it into her carry-on. As she did so, he took the bag and hefted it onto his lap. He pushed the magazine aside and pulled out one of her zippered makeup pouches. Inside was a small aluminum snap case. He opened it just enough to show her four joints.

"Are you totally insane! Jesus!" she seethed under her breath.

"The genius of it, Libby," he reminded her calmly, "is that no one brings dope *in*to the Caribbean, right?"

She had a good look around the lobby while David checked them into the Beach Banner Inn. If you'd just read about the place in a travel magazine, she mused, you'd say no way. It sounded like shag carpets, polyester blankets, plastic water glasses in the bathroom. But this was quite classy, she decided, the oversize bouquets of fresh flowers, really good-looking people having espresso. The women were mostly in white, she observed, with gold accessories, so that was going to be no problem. She agreed with David's judgment. Why go to a top-of-the-line Hyatt or Sheraton, where you get the heavy terry-cloth robes, the turn-down service, when for 40 percent less you get what you actually need? He had enumerated: a view of the water, cable access, firm pillows, the right drinks in the minibar (he'd asked which labels, he said), and then something nice, like two sinks. And these people didn't skimp, he emphasized, with cheap necessities like wire hangers and little soap bars. He'd asked.

He did know how to handle it all, she reflected.

"What I like with him," she'd told her friend Helena, "is that this guy who makes like a hundred and sixteen thousand dollars a year goes to the trouble to actually check everything out, to spend the money smartly, you know, not just throw it at travel agents, whatever it costs, who cares. One thousand five hundred for a week in the Caribbean, Brad told me, and most of that went for the room, with the big towels and the turn-down service. Meals extra. That was Brad. For the same money David gets the hotel, plus a three-star restaurant, all that in a plan, plus five days—five entire days—on a private dive boat. Plus he sent flowers when I got certified to dive."

"So is this guy married?" asked Helena.

"Are you totally insane?"

While she unpacked, David phoned his mother in New Jersey and Libby heard his side of it.

"Hey, Mom."

"_____."

"Yeah, because you weren't home and you didn't have the machine on."

"_____."

"How's Dad, how's he getting on?"

"_____."

"Well, it's going to get better. I know that. Listen, I wanted to see how you were. I'm going to call you in a few days."

"_____."

"I'm out of the country, Mom. I'm traveling. I'll call in a few days. I love you. Him, too."

"_____."

"Okay, bye."

David stood still awhile, holding the receiver, his finger depressing the disconnect bar, as though considering another call. Then he cradled the receiver, looking tired.

While they were dressing for dinner she noticed he'd brought all new clothes, new slacks, new shirts.

"You try on all your clothes?" he asked her. When she looked back at him blankly he said, "Lots of people buy clothes for a vacation, but they don't try them on before they leave. They end up with things that don't fit, or they don't match, or there's an imperfection. You bring any new clothes?"

"Well, I already had almost everything I needed—"

"Okay, so it's not that special to you."

"Except the Hilfiger windbreaker you got me. And I got some underwear."

She wished right away she hadn't said it. He hunched over

and began to imitate a crowing rooster flapping its wings and then broke into an imitation of a matador's capework, daring the bull to charge.

The restaurant was called Michael's. He'd gotten them a table near a window so they could see the sun set. She gave him an approving look.

When she reached for her menu, he waved her off. "I'll order," he told her. "If you don't know—I don't know, maybe you know—but if you don't know how to order food and wine in a foreign country, you can screw it up. You don't want that. Besides, in some of these places you have to be able to read *through* the menu, you know, to what they're actually saying. You gotta put the French aside."

When the waiter came, David ordered oysters for both of them and a bottle of cabernet sauvignon.

"A cabernet, sir?"

"Yes."

"Very good, sir."

"And I'll go with the marlin and, for her, the grouper. Now this is local, right?"

"Yes sir. We purchased it this afternoon on the dock."

"But, instead of the rémoulade, the mango and chili deal, we'll have peas. Fresh peas mixed with carrots. Can you do that?"

"Of course, sir."

"And with dinner we'll have a California chardonnay. Let's see if you've got a Chalone here." He picked up the wine list.

"Would monsieur like to try perhaps a Riesling or a Pinot Gris with the fish?"

"No. This Chalone here will be great."

They ate in silence. She always found this the hardest part. She felt stupid, that she had nothing to say. She thought about the Bob Marley tape, but she'd forgotten to listen to it. She remembered some guy in the news a while back, maybe in Haiti, but not what that was about. Were they coffee growers on San Carlos? Her job. Boring. David said the place she worked, a psychiatric clinic, was interesting because more and more people were actually crazy, but he said the doctors were all losers—"dogheads," he called them—because they had no Web sites. "Sooner or later," he told her, "every*body* and every*thing* is going to be on-line.

"If you want to make yourself some money," he advised, "look deep into your business—step one. Step two, upgrade. Everywhere. For example, with the Web sites, you've already got psychiatric profiles, I've read up on them. You can match those profiles to standard kinds of treatment, therapy, whatever, and some people will be able to cure themselves, right off the Net. You laugh, but it's true. If you have correct information and you apply yourself, you can do anything. Up until now, too much information has been in the hands of too few people."

She didn't think it would work, but she hadn't wanted to get into it with him.

She was watching the sunset and wondering if this was when you saw the green flash.

"Are you married?" she asked him.

"Married. Are you kidding?"

· · ·

She wanted to try the sorbet with fresh guava for dessert, but he ordered Key lime pie.

"Dairy," he cautioned her. "Never order dairy in the tropics."

After the meal he asked for Courvoisier on the deck and ordered amaretto for her.

She thought the stars were beautiful. She wanted to lie in his arms, but he hardly looked at her. He sipped a second Courvoisier and nodded at people who walked past, as though they were all in on the same arrangement. When women with large breasts came by, he stared at them until they passed.

Their room was nonsmoking, but he said that didn't apply to incense and lit two tapers. She wasn't sure.

"Nah, nah. Didn't you ever get in a cab with these people? They all have twenty air fresheners going, they love this stuff. It's cigarettes. Cigarettes are the problem."

He was watching her get undressed with a look that made her uncomfortable. She went into the bathroom to change. She had begun to worry a little about sex. In the beginning it had been great, but then he wanted to try things which, even though she had heard of them, seemed strange, even if you were in love. He told her he wanted to tie her to the bed and spank her with a grade-school ruler. And he kept suggesting that she shave her pubic hair off. When they made love and he rolled off and went to sleep and she told him that wasn't making love, he said it was. "You satisfy me so much," he explained, "I go straight into dream sleep, right into REM sleep."

When she came out of the bathroom in her short night-gown, she saw he'd turned out all the lights.

Learning to dive was the big issue, Libby knew, for their trip. She had worked diligently at it, getting the theory down as well as all the skills—buddy breathing, neutral buoyancy, mask clearing. David, who was certified to the level of rescue diver, had chosen her training program, but she went by herself to the classes, and her instructors told her she was one of the best they ever had. And they said they envied her the trip to San Carlos, a little-dived locale that was getting a reputation as the place to go in the eastern Caribbean.

After breakfast, after they'd gotten all their gear down to the dock, David found he'd left his gold ear stud in the room. He asked her to go back for it. He was fanatical, she'd learned, about his ear studs. He tried to explain to her one time what the different occasions were, for the silver one with the miniature rose, the turquoise one, the one with the diamond out of his grandmother's engagement ring, and the plain gold one. He said he wouldn't dive without the gold one, but she couldn't keep it all straight. It was like the time he tried to explain to her why some baseball player had to eat some combination of Kentucky Fried Chicken exactly two hours before every game.

When she got back with the stud, David was arguing with the boatman. It was an open twenty-foot skiff, a Boston Whaler with two big engines that looked brand-new and eight dive tanks mounted in a wooden rack like wine bottles. David was leaning against the steering console with his lime-green wraparound sunglasses and holding his chest out, she noticed, more than he usually did.

"You gotta know some places, man, places nobody's been before. I mean, that's the deal here, right, with a private boat?"

"Everyting be good, mon. It be good. You gon like everyting."

She felt drawn immediately to the boatman's lean body, like one of the jacaranda trees in full bloom. She had never seen blacker skin, a more compact yet muscular torso. Every muscle, every sinew, was tight under his tight skin. His lips were full, the veins in his hands prominent, his bare shoulders square. But for a missing tooth, his broken and discolored fingernails and callused feet, she thought him the handsomest man she'd ever seen. She hoped he'd be nice. And maybe give David a little grief.

"So, Esteban," David was saying while they were preparing to cast off, "let me get you around on this, man. We've got to go to at least a couple of undived places in the next few days. All right? I've got to be able to tell people we were the first on a couple of these places, you know what I'm saying?" David had taken a fifty out of the envelope with the $5,000. Holding it up, he said, "Am I getting through here, Esteban? Do we have a deal?"

She was embarrassed when he did this, his De Niro imitation.

"Okay, mon," said Esteban. "We hit some places. But I be pickin dem, because some places, de are no good to go. You know?"

"Yeah, I get it. Currents."

"It ain no currents, ma frien."

"Drop 'em and light 'em, Esteban, and let's get out of here."

His Kevin Costner, she thought, as David swung around by the steering console, folded his arms and gazed out toward the channel.

"Why did you show him all that money?" she whispered later. "Don't you think that was really risky, letting him see, and people all around?"

"What he knows now is, there's the possibility of a big tip if we see some cool stuff. The money's totally safe. He's just a chained dog at the resort. He's going to try something?"

The boat idled out of the small harbor and into the channel between San Carlos and Itesea to the south. When Esteban brought the throttles up full, the boat got up on plane and began cracking the flat swell at twenty-four knots, headed southeast for an area Esteban said was called Los Pachucos, because of the sharks. The morning sun lit the water dark blue over the deep channel and then a paler blue and turquoise as they came back to the shallower water. With her polarized glasses Libby could see the reefs flashing by under the boat and swarms of fish bolting. David leaned over to reassure her, to say the sharks would be no problem.

Esteban cut the throttles and shifted into neutral but didn't drop his anchor. He told them anchors damage the coral. Instead, he said, he'd follow their bubbles, and the most important thing for them to remember was to surface away from the boat, alongside him if they could, but never near the engines. It was very important.

While they were pulling on their dive gear, she asked Esteban about the other island, Itesea.

"Dat da military, miss. You don' wan mess wid dem. We don' go over dat way, that is what I am telling your mon here. Plenty good places to dive, but not over dat way."

Plunging through the surface of the water made her euphoric, feeling the powerful, effervescent stroke of her body, the weightlessness of astronauts. She was so happy entering that transparent world she reached out to high-five David. When their hands collided awkwardly, she had the momentary sensation she could have done this alone, that she did not need him. The passing streamers of brightly colored damselfish, of French grunts and sergeant majors, huge stingrays rising slowly, regally, from camouflage on the sand flats, the way tiny nudibranchs glistened like flower buds on the coral heads all made her light-headed with satisfaction, a sense of having chosen right. Brad, she remembered, hadn't even thought to get them certified, and then he'd been too cheap to pay for the resort course. He wanted to surf.

They moved to a new area of Los Pachucos and dove again and then had lunch. She was disappointed when Esteban confirmed that he had no picture guides aboard for the underwater life.

"Any fish you tell me, I know dat," he said, laughing. "But people, de don' eat dat other. Gotta eat, you know." He waited. He chucked his chin at her and winked. "I get de guides for you tomorrow," he said.

David had come up from his second dive with two large conchs, thinking they would bring them back to the hotel and have someone prepare them for dinner, but Esteban made him drop them overboard.

"It's illegal, mon. De never let you anywhere near de hotel wid it. Put it over."

"Don't you have a few pals," challenged David, "people who know how to do this? I mean, we don't have to take them to the hotel, you could take them somewhere else, and we could come by and eat, at your place maybe. It'd make a good story, you know what I mean?"

"Put dem over, mon. Drop dem in."

"You're not a get-ahead guy, Esteban," complained David. He let the conchs slip over the side, where they fell quickly through the water, rocking toward the bottom like leaves from a tree. "But I like you." He gave Esteban his De Niro smile.

Lunch was fried fillets of Atlantic cod on stale white rolls with organic chips, a banana each, and Blue Sky cream sodas. David winked knowingly at Libby, as if to say, You have to expect some breakdown in quality somewhere along the way. Still, she couldn't believe it. Salt cod?

While they digested the meal, she and David stretched out on lounge mats in the bow and held hands. She had to flick his other hand away a few times, with Esteban there. He got up and got his biography of Robert Moses out of his dive bag and finished the last twenty pages.

"Handle a spliff, Esteban?"

"Not today, mon."

"You're cool, Esteban, you know?" He inhaled the joint and gazed at the passing water. "That's good, about the conchs, no toking while you're navigating. But you know, man, I'm gonna tell you something. You need to evolve—you know what I mean?—evolve to get ahead here. You own this boat?"

"It's ma boat."

"Ever think about owning maybe two or three boats? Getting some of your buddies to work for you, booking pax yourself in the States, not through the hotel? You into the Net? You could get a Web site. I could set it up. You could pull in a lot of money."

"I'm okay like dis. Ma boat, it's all paid up. I'm good."

"Well you gotta get better, Esteban, or what are you here for? Right?"

"I be tinkin about it, den."

They cruised on, watching white pelicans skimming inches above the water and the reef pattern quivering below sheets of broken light on the surface.

"Ma fatha, he own dis boat," Esteban began. "He fish, all true here, all di wata here, and out der, way out der, for marlin, for swordfish. De all gone now. Just de little ones lef. He was de fishermon, you know, and I am de divin mon. So we be makin de changes, mon, we be gettin on. Evolvin."

Esteban turned around to gaze astern. On the northwest horizon he saw the glitter of a boat moving fast toward Itesea. He shook his head with a wry smile and idled on.

"This looks good, Esteban my man. Let's jump in here," said David.

"We go on a little bit. It be betta. We comin a place call Zanja de Bacalao."

Esteban turned to look for the boat again. As he watched, it peeled away from the horizon and headed toward them. Esteban swung his boat all the way around to the north and brought the engines up to full throttle. The Whaler came up on plane and Libby sat up and looked around. David took a tight grip on the steering console.

"What's up here, dude?"

"I takin a precaution, mon. You see dot? Dot's what I tellin you. You never know out here anymore."

The other boat was driving toward them on a line to intercept. Esteban could tell it was fast, a cigarette boat. "Could be de military," he said. "Tings always changin."

They could see the low coast of San Carlos looming beyond the bow and hear the smack of the skiff on the dazzling water.

"You may haf to buy us outta dis one, mon."

David kept his eyes on the boat, closing fast, but said nothing.

"You put dat money you got in de pocket of your BC, mon, and you leave a little in de envelope, cause if we haf to pay, de gonna want it all."

"I'm cool."

David split the money, putting $4,500 in his buoyancy control vest, leaving $500 in the envelope.

"What's happening," asked Libby, pulling a linen wrap around herself and trying to stand steady on the pounding deck.

"Military, maybe," said David. "We might have gotten in too close to Itesea here, so these guys could be hard-asses about it. Maybe we're going to have to buy our way out."

The boat closed on them like a barracuda, then roared along parallel with the Whaler. The driver indicated to Esteban with a hand gesture to shut it down. Esteban thought to just hold his course for San Carlos until he saw the guns. He throttled back, and then the big boat, twice the length of his, was wallowing alongside, its exhaust guttering as it rolled in its own wake. The boat had a low cabin forward, a sleek white hull, and no insignia. The barefoot man at the helm had dreadlocks and dark glasses and was wearing a dirty pair of pale blue trousers. Two other men stood braced at the boat's gunwale, looking them over. One of them wore four watches, two on each wrist.

"This is not the military," said Esteban.

The shirtless man in madras shorts raised a .9 mm Glock and began spraying Esteban. The first bullet tore through his left triceps, the second, third, fourth, and fifth hit nothing, the sixth perforated his spleen, the seventh and eighth hit nothing, the ninth hit the console, sending electrical sparks up, the tenth went through his right palm, the next four went into the air, the fifteenth tore his left ear away, the sixteenth ricocheted off the sixth cervical vertebrae and drove down through his heart, exiting through his abdomen and lodging in his foot. The seventeenth, eighteenth, and nineteenth went out over the water.

David watched Esteban shudder and fall like an imploded vase.

The driver dropped white fenders over the side and powered the boat in closer. The other two snagged bow and stern cleats with a pole and gaff, snugged the boats together and tied off. Then both jumped on board. David raised his hands to say he would be no problem, take whatever. The first man to reach him seemed uncoordinated, as if he were drunk, but his first punch broke David's nose and then he pummeled him backward over a seat, and when he fell the man slammed him repeatedly in the head with a dive regulator.

The other man, who had a barbed-wire tattoo wrapped around his chest, plowed through the contents of the dive bags. He pitched the tin of marijuana to the first man. When he found the envelope he ripped the money out and stuffed the bills in his swim trunks. Libby stood in the back of the skiff, crying, with her hands over her mouth. The man in the other boat glanced at her, but she could not see his eyes. Once in a while he brought his throttle up to steady the boats on the swell.

The man with the chest tattoo was ransacking the many pockets of the dive bags in a fury. The other one had yanked David's gold Rolex Submariner off and was kicking at him to keep him still while he adjusted it on his wrist. The man in the swim trunks threw the doors of the steering console open, emptied out the lunch locker and opened the fish wells, until nothing around him stood unopened. He gazed at the man in the other boat, waiting for instructions. The whites of his eyes were marred with many tiny exploded blood vessels. The man on the other boat shrugged, as if it hadn't been worth it.

"You got more money, sweetheart?" said the man in the boat.

Libby rushed to the BC, tore open the Velcro pocket, and held out the $4,500.

"Nice, very nice," said the man in the boat. "We goin now," he shouted to the other two. "Kill dem."

"Oh no, oh no, oh no," Libby murmured.

The man with the tattoo hit her in the neck with his fist, knocking her into the engines, and then banged her head on the deck of the boat until she was unconscious. He laid her over the back of a bench seat and raped her. It took him a long time and in the middle of it he lit a cigarette. The man with the watches trussed David with monofilament fishing line and choked him to death while he raped him.

When they were finished, the man in the boat hoisted over three pairs of concrete footings. The others tied the bodies to metal straps on the footings, rolled them over the side and dropped the blocks in the water. Tied to the two white people were their dive bags, zippered shut with their belongings. They handed the dive tanks and other equipment across to the driver, who helped the man with the tattoo board and then they cast off.

The man with the watches used Esteban's deck brushes to clean the boat, washing the blood into the engine well. Then he brought the throttles up on the idling engines and turned the skiff in a skidding arc after the other boat. The water in the engine well flushed out through the scuppers and Esteban's Whaler came up on plane, following the other boat toward Itesea.

A few miles east a man was fishing for grouper. He had caught only two among the reefs since sunup, not such a good day, but they pay very good at the dock, he thought, and whatever he brought in they always bought. He was thinking how he liked that, coming in with the fish at the end of the day. The guests from the hotel always liked it that he was wearing the Docker cut-offs his wife had fixed up and his J. Crew shirt or the shirt with the black Labrador. They liked his fish and his accent. They liked his laugh. He only had to get more fish, he thought, more fish and it was going to be good.

He held the baited hook up before his eyes. His father had taught him how to make the tiny marks he had cut in its shank, and he stared hard at them now and said, "Do your work."

He flipped the baited hook overboard and watched the line spool out under his thumb.

The Mappist

When I was an undergraduate at Brown I came across a book called *The City of Ascensions,* about Bogotá. I knew nothing of Bogotá, but I felt the author had captured its essence. My view was that Onesimo Peña had not written a travel book but a work about the soul of Bogotá. Even if I were to read it later in life, I thought, I would not be able to get all Peña meant in a single reading. I looked him up at the library but he had apparently written no other books, at least not any in English.

In my senior year I discovered a somewhat better known book, *The City of Trembling Leaves,* by Walter Van Tilburg Clark, about Reno, Nevada. I liked it, but it did not have the superior depth, the integration of Peña's work. Peña, you had the feeling, could walk you through the warrens of Bogotá without a map and put your hands directly on the vitality of any modern century—the baptismal registries of a particular cathedral, a cornerstone that had been taken from one building to be used in another, a London plane tree planted by Bolívar. He had such a command of the idiom of this city, and the book itself demonstrated such complex linkages, it was easy to believe Peña had no other subject, that he could have written nothing else. I believed this was so until I read *The City of Floating Sand* a year later, a book about Cape Town, and then a book about Djakarta, called *The City of Frangipani.* Though the former was by one Frans Haartman and the latter by a Jemboa Tran, each had the distinctive organic layering of the Peña book, and I felt certain they'd been written by the same man.

A national library search through the University of Michigan, where I had gone to work on a master's degree in geography, produced hundreds of books with titles similar to these. I had to know whether Peña had written any others and so read or skimmed perhaps thirty of those I got through interlibrary loan. Some, though wretched, were strange enough to be engaging; others were brilliant but not in the way of Peña. I ended up ordering copies of five I believed Peña had written, books about Perth, Lagos, Tokyo, Venice, and Boston, the last a volume by William Smith Everett called *The City of Cod.*

Who Peña actually was I could not then determine. Letters to publishers eventually led me to a literary agency in New York where I was told that the author did not wish to be known. I pressed for information about what else he might have written, inquired whether he was still alive (the book about Venice had been published more than fifty years before), but got nowhere.

As a doctoral student at Duke I made the seven Peña books the basis of a dissertation. I wanted to show in a series of city maps, based on all the detail in Peña's descriptions, what a brilliant exegesis of the social dynamics of these cities he had achieved. My maps showed, for example, how water moved through Djakarta, not just municipal water but also trucked water and, street by street, the flow of rainwater. And how road building in Cape Town reflected the policy of apartheid.

I received quite a few compliments on the work, but I knew the maps did not make apparent the hard, translucent jewel of integration that was each Peña book. I had only created some illustrations, however well done. But had I known whether he was alive or where he lived, I would still have sent him a copy out of a sense of collegiality and respect.

After I finished the dissertation I moved my wife and three young children to Brookline, a suburb of Boston, and set up a practice as a restoration geographer. Fifteen years later I embarked on my fourth or fifth trip to Tokyo as a consultant to a planning firm there, and one evening I took a train out to Chiyoda-ku to visit bookstores in an area called Jimbocho. Just down the street from a bridge over the Kanda River is the Sanseido Book Store, a regular haunt by then for me. Up on the fifth floor I bought two translations of books by Japanese writers on the Asian architectual response to topography in mountain cities. I was exiting the store on the ground floor, a level given over entirely to maps, closing my coat against the spring night, when I happened to spot the kanji for "Tokyo" on a tier of drawers. I opened one of them to browse. Toward the bottom of a second drawer, I came upon a set of maps that seemed vaguely familiar, though the entries were all in kanji. After a few minutes of leafing through, it dawned on me that they bore a resemblance to the maps I had done as a student at Duke. I was considering buying one of them as a memento when I caught a name in English in the corner—Corlis Benefideo. It appeared there on every map.

I stared at that name a long while, and I began to consider what you also may be thinking. I bought all thirteen maps. Even without language to identify information in the keys, even without titles, I could decipher what the mapmaker was up to. One designated areas prone to flooding as water from the Sumida River backed up through the city's storm drains. Another showed the location of all shops dealing in Edo Period manuscripts and artwork. Another, using small pink arrows, showed the point of view of each of Hiroshige's famous One Hundred Views. Yet another showed, in six time-sequenced panels, the rise and decline of horse barns in the city.

My office in Boston was fourteen hours behind me, so I had to leave a message for my assistant, asking him to look up Corlis Benefideo's name. I gave him some contacts at map libraries I used regularly, and asked him to call me back as soon as he had anything, no matter the hour. He called at three a.m. to say that Corlis Benefideo had worked as a mapmaker for the U.S. Coast and Geodetic Survey in Washington from 1932 until 1958, and that he was going to fax me some more information.

I dressed and went down to the hotel lobby to wait for the faxes and read them while I stood there. Benefideo was born in Fargo, North Dakota, in 1912. He went to work for the federal government straight out of Grinnell College during the Depression and by 1940 was traveling to various places—Venice, Bogotá, Lagos—in an exchange program. In 1958 he went into private practice as a cartographer in Chicago. His main source of income at that time appeared to be from the production of individualized site maps for large estate homes being built along the North Shore of Lake Michigan. The maps were bound in oversize books, twenty by thirty inches, and showed the vegetation, geology, hydrology, biology, and even archaeology of each site. They were subcontracted for under several architects.

Benefideo's Chicago practice closed in 1975. The fax said nothing more was known of his work history, and that he was not listed in any Chicago area phone books, nor with any professional organizations. I faxed back to my office, asking them to check phone books in Fargo, in Washington, D.C., and around Grinnell, Iowa—Des Moines and those towns. And asking them to try to find someone at what was now the National Geodetic Survey who might have known Benefideo or who could provide some detail.

When I came back to the hotel the following afternoon, there was another fax. No luck with the phone books, I read, but I could call a Maxwell Abert at the National Survey who'd worked with Benefideo. I waited the necessary few hours for the time change and called.

Abert said he had overlapped with Benefideo for one year, 1958, and though Benefideo had left voluntarily, it wasn't his idea.

"What you had to understand about Corlis," he said, "was

that he was a patriot. Now, that word today, I don't know, means maybe nothing, but Corlis felt this very strong commitment to his country, and to a certain kind of mapmaking, and he and the Survey just ended up on a collision course. The way Corlis worked, you see, the way he approached things, slowed down the production of maps. That wasn't any good from a bureaucratic point of view. He couldn't give up being comprehensive, you understand, and they just didn't know what to do with him."

"What happened to him?"

"Well, the man spoke five or six languages, and he had both the drafting ability and the conceptual skill of a first-rate cartographer, so the government should have done something to keep the guy—and he was also very loyal—but they didn't. Oh, his last year they created a project for him, but it was temporary. He saw they didn't want him. He moved to Chicago—but you said you knew that."

"Mmm. Do you know where he went after Chicago?"

"I do. He went to Fargo. And that's the last I know. I wrote him there until about 1985—he'd have been in his seventies—and then the last letter came back 'no forwarding address.' So that's the last I heard. I believe he must have died. He'd be, what, eighty-eight now."

"What was the special project?"

"Well Corlis, you know, he was like something out of a WPA project, like Dorothea Lange, Walker Evans and James Agee and them, people that had this sense of America as a country under siege, undergoing a trial during the Depression, a society that needed its dignity back. Corlis believed that in order to effect any political or social change, you had to know exactly what you were talking about. You had to know what the country itself—the ground, the real thing, not some political abstraction—was all about. So he proposed this series of forty-eight sets of maps—this was just before Alaska and Hawaii came in—a series for each state that would show the geology and hydrology, where the water was, you know, and the botany and biology, and the history of the place from Native American times.

"Well, a hundred people working hundred-hour weeks for a decade might get it all down, you know—it was monumental, what he was proposing. But to keep him around, to have him in the office, the Survey created this pilot project so he could come up with an approach that might get it done in a reasonable amount of time—why, I don't know; the government works on most things forever—but that's what he did. I never saw the results, but if you ever wanted to see disillusionment in a man, you should have seen Corlis in those last months. He tried congressmen, he tried senators, he tried other people in Commerce, he tried everybody, but I think they all had the same sense of him, that he was an obstructionist. They'd eat a guy like that alive on the Hill today, the same way. He just wasn't very practical. But he was a good man."

I got the address in Fargo and thanked Mr. Abert. It turned out to be where Benefideo's parents had lived until they died. The house was sold in 1985. And that was that.

When I returned to Boston I reread *The City of Ascensions*. It's a beautiful book, so tender toward the city, and proceeding on the assumption that Bogotá was the living idea of its inhabitants. I thought Benefideo's books would make an exceptional subject for a senior project in history or geography, and wanted to suggest it to my older daughter, Stephanie. How, I might ask her, do we cultivate people like Corlis Benefideo? Do they all finally return to the rural districts from which they come, unable or unwilling to fully adapt to the goals, the tone, of a progressive society? Was Corlis familiar with the work of Lewis Mumford? Would you call him a populist?

Stephanie, about to finish her junior year at Bryn Mawr, had an interest in cities and geography, but I didn't know how to follow up on this with her. Her interests were there in spite of my promotions.

One morning, several months after I got back from Tokyo, I walked into the office and saw a note in the center of my desk, a few words from my diligent assistant. It was Benefideo's address—Box 117, Garrison, North Dakota 58540. I got out the office atlas. Garrison is halfway between Minot and Bismarck, just north of Lake Sakakawea. No phone.

I wrote him a brief letter, saying I'd recently bought a set of his maps in Tokyo, asking if he was indeed the author of the books, and telling him how much I admired them and that I had based my Ph.D. dissertation on them. I praised the integrity of the work he had done, and said I was intrigued by his last Survey project, and would also like to see one of the Chicago publications sometime.

A week later I got a note. "Dear Mr. Trevino," it read.

I appreciate your kind words about my work. I am still at it. Come for a visit if you wish. I will be back from a trip in late September, so the first week of October would be fine. Sincerely, Corlis Benefideo.

I located a motel in Garrison, got plane tickets to Bismarck, arranged a rental car, and then wrote Mr. Benefideo and told him I was coming, and that if he would send me his street address I would be at his door at nine a.m. on October second. The address he sent, 15088 State Highway 37, was a few miles east of Garrison. A hand-rendered map in colored pencil, which made tears well up in my eyes, showed how to get to the house, which lay a ways off the road in a grove of ash trees he had sketched.

The days of waiting made me anxious and aware of my vulnerability. I asked both my daughters and my son if they wanted to go. No, school was starting, they wanted to be with their friends. My wife debated, then said no. She thought this was something that would go best if I went alone.

Corlis was straddling the sill of his door as I drove in to his yard. He wore a pair of khaki trousers, a khaki shirt, and a khaki ball cap. He was about five foot six and lean. Though spry, he showed evidence of arthritis and the other infirmities of age in his walk and handshake.

During breakfast I noticed a set of *The City of* books on his shelves. There were eight, which meant I'd missed one. After breakfast he asked if I'd brought any binoculars, and whether I'd be interested in visiting a wildlife refuge a few miles away off the Bismarck highway, to watch ducks and geese coming in from Canada. He made a picnic lunch and we drove over and had a fine time. I had no binoculars with me, and little interest in the birds to start with, but with his guidance and animation I came to appreciate the place. We saw more than a million birds that day, he said.

When we got back to the house I asked if I could scan his bookshelves while he fixed dinner. He had thousands of books, a significant number of them in Spanish and French and some in Japanese. (The eighth book was called *The City of Geraniums*, about Lima.) On the walls of a large room that incorporated the kitchen and dining area was perhaps the most astonishing collection of hand-drawn maps I had ever seen outside a library. Among them were two of McKenzie's map sketches from his exploration of northern Canada; four of FitzRoy's coastal elevations from Chile, made during the voyage with Darwin; one of Humboldt's maps of the Orinoco; and a half-dozen sketches of the Thames docks by Samuel Pepys.

Mr. Benefideo made us a dinner of canned soup, canned meat, and canned vegetables. For dessert he served fresh fruit, some store-bought cookies, and instant coffee. I studied him at the table. His forehead was high, and a prominent jaw and large nose further elongated his face. His eyes were pale blue, his skin burnished and dark, like a Palermo fisherman's. His ears flared slightly. His hair, still black on top, was close-cropped. There was little in the face but the alertness of the eyes to give you a sense of the importance of his work.

After dinner our conversation took a more satisfying turn. He had discouraged conversation while we were watching the birds, and he had seemed disinclined to talk while he was rid-ing in the car. Our exchanges around dinner—which was quick—were broken up by its preparation and by clearing the table. A little to my surprise, he offered me Mexican tequila after the meal. I declined, noticing the bottle had no label, but sat with him on the porch while he drank.

Yes, he said, he'd used the pen names to keep the government from finding out what else he'd been up to in those cities. And yes, the experience with the Survey had made him a little bitter, but it had also opened the way to other things. His work in Chicago had satisfied him—the map sets for the estate architects and their wealthy clients, he made clear, were a minor thing; his real business in those years was in other countries, where hand-drawn and hand-colored maps still were welcome and enthused over. The estate map books, however, had allowed him to keep his hand in on the kind of work he wanted to pursue more fully one day. In 1975 he came back to Fargo to take care of his parents. When they died he sold the house and moved to Garrison. He had a government pension—when he said this he flicked his eyebrows, as though in the end he had gotten the best of the government. He had a small income from his books, he told me, mostly the foreign editions. And he had put some money away, so he'd been able to buy this place.

"What are you doing now?"

"The North Dakota series, the work I proposed in Washington in fifty-seven."

"The hydrological maps, the biological maps?"

"Yes. I subdivided the state into different sections, the actual number depending on whatever scale I needed for that subject. I've been doing them for fifteen years now, a thousand six hundred and fifty-one maps. I want to finish them, you know, so that if anyone ever wants to duplicate the work, they'll have a good idea of how to go about it."

He gazed at me in a slightly disturbing, almost accusatory way.

"Are you going to donate the maps, then, to a place where they can be studied?"

"North Dakota Museum of Art, in Grand Forks."

"Did you never marry, never have children?"

"I'm not sure, you know. No, I never married—I asked a few times, but was turned down. I didn't have the features, I think, and, early on, no money. Afterward, I developed a way of life that was really too much my own on a day-to-day basis. But, you know, I've been the beneficiary of great kindness in my life, and some of it has come from women who were, or are, very dear to me. Do you know what I mean?"

"Yes, I do."

"As for children, I think maybe there are one or two. In Bogotá. Venice. Does it shock you?"

"People are not shocked by things like this anymore, Mister Benefideo."

"That's too bad. I am. I have made my peace with it, though. Would you like to see the maps?"

"The Dakota series?"

Mr. Benefideo took me to a second large room with more stunning maps on the walls, six or eight tiers of large map drawers, and a worktable the perimeter of which was stained with hundreds of shades of watercolors surrounding a gleaming white area about three feet square. He turned on some track lighting which made the room very bright and pointed me to a swivel stool in front of an empty table, a smooth, broad surface of some waxed and dark wood.

From an adjacent drawer he pulled out a set of large maps, which he laid in front of me.

"As you go through, swing them to the side there. I'll restack them."

The first map was of ephemeral streams in the northeast quadrant of the state.

"These streams," he pointed out, "run only during wet periods, some but once in twenty years. Some don't have any names."

The information was strikingly presented and beautifully drawn. The instruction you needed to get oriented—where the Red River was, where the county lines were—was just enough, so it barely impinged on the actual subject matter of the map. The balance was perfect.

The next map showed fence lines, along the Missouri River in a central part of the state.

"These are done at twenty-year intervals, going back to eighteen forty. Fences are like roads, they proliferate. They're never completely removed."

The following map was a geological rendering of McIntosh County's bedrock geology. As I took in the shape and colors, the subdivided shades of purple and green and blue, Mr. Benefideo slid a large hand-colored transparency across the sheet, a soil map of the same area. You could imagine looking down through a variety of soil types to the bedrock below.

"Or," he said, and slid an opaque map with the same information across in front of me, the yellows and browns of a dozen silts, clays, and sands.

The next sheet was of eighteenth- and nineteenth-century foot trails in the western half of the state.

"But how did you compile this information?"

"Inspection and interviews. Close personal observation and talking with long-term residents. It's a hard thing, really, to erase a trail. A lot of information can be recovered if you stay at it."

When he placed the next map in front of me, the summer distribution of Swainson's hawks, and then slid in next to it a map showing the overlapping summer distribution of its main prey species, the Richardson ground squirrel, the precision and revelation were too much for me.

I turned to face him. "I've never seen anything that even approaches this, this"—my gesture across the surface of the table included everything. "It's not just the information, or the execution—I mean, the technique is flawless, the watercoloring, your choice of scale—but it's like the books, there's so much more."

"That's the idea, don't you think, Mister Trevino?"

"Of course, but nobody has the time for this kind of fieldwork anymore."

"That's unfortunate, because this information is what we need, you know. This shows history and how people fit the places they occupy. It's about what gets erased and what comes to replace it. These maps reveal the foundations beneath the ephemera."

"What about us, though?" I blurted, resisting his pronouncement. "In the books, in *City in Aspic* in particular, there is such a palpable love of human life in the cities, and here—"

"I do not have to live up to the history of Venice, Mister Trevino," he interrupted, "but I am obliged to shoulder the history of my own country. I could show you here the whole coming and going of the Mandan nation, wiped out in eighteen thirty-seven by a smallpox epidemic. I could show you how the arrival of German and Scandinavian farmers changed the composition of the topsoil, and the places where Charles Bodmer painted, and the evolution of red-light districts in Fargo—all that with pleasure. I've nothing against human passion, human longing. What I oppose is blind devotion to progress, and the venality of material wealth. If we're going to trade the priceless for the common, I want to know exactly what the terms are."

I had no response. His position was as difficult to assail as it would be to promote.

"You mean," I finally ventured, "that someone else will have to do the maps that show the spread of the Wal-Mart empire in North Dakota."

"I won't be doing those."

His tone was assertive but not testy. He wasn't even seeking my agreement.

"My daughter," I said, changing the subject, "wants to be an environmental historian. She has a good head for it, and I know she's interested—she wants to discover the kind of information you need to have to build a stable society. I'm sure it comes partly from looking at what's already there, as you suggest, like the birds this morning, how that movement, those movements, might determine the architecture of a society. I'm wondering—could I ever send her out? Maybe to help? Would you spend a few days with her?"

"I'd be glad to speak with her," he said, after considering the question. "I'd train her, if it came to that."

"Thank you."

He began squaring the maps up to place them back in the drawer.

"You know, Mister Trevino—Phillip, if I may, and you may call me Corlis—the question is about you, really." He shut the drawer and gestured me toward the door of the room, which he closed behind us.

"You represent a questing but lost generation of people. I think you know what I mean. You made it clear this morning, talking nostalgically about my books, that you think an elegant order has disappeared, something that shows the way." We were standing at the corner of the dining table with our hands on the chair backs. "It's wonderful, of course, that you brought your daughter into our conversation tonight, and certainly we're both going to have to depend on her, on her thinking. But the real question, now, is what will *you* do? Because you can't expect her to take up something you wish for yourself, a way of seeing the world. You send her here, if it turns out to be what she wants, but don't make the mistake of thinking you, or I or anyone, knows how the world is meant to work. The world is a miracle, unfolding in the pitch dark. We're lighting candles. Those maps—they are my candles. And I can't extinguish them for anyone."

He crossed to his shelves and took down his copy of *The City of Geraniums*. He handed it to me and we went to the door.

"If you want to come back in the morning for breakfast, please do. Or, there is a cafe, the Dogwood, next to the motel. It's good. However you wish."

We said good night and I moved out through pools of dark beneath the ash trees to where I'd parked the car. I set the book on the seat opposite and started the engine. The headlights swept the front of the house as I turned past it, catching the salute of his hand, and then he was gone.

I inverted the image of the map from his letter in my mind and began driving south to the highway. After a few moments I turned off the headlights and rolled down the window. I listened to the tires crushing gravel in the roadbed. The sound of it helped me hold the road, together with instinct and the memory of earlier having driven it. I felt the volume of space beneath the clear, star-ridden sky, and moved over the dark prairie like a barn-bound horse.